A New Family for the Cowboy

Christian Contemporary Western Romance

Brush Creek Cowboys Romance
Book Four

Liz Isaacson

Copyright © 2020 by Elana Johnson, writing as Liz Isaacson

All rights reserved.

No part of this book may be reproduced in any form or by any electronic or mechanical means, including information storage and retrieval systems, without written permission from the author, except for the use of brief quotations in a book review.

ISBN-13: 978-1638760849

"For therefore we both labour and suffer reproach, because we trust in the living God, who is the Savior of all men, specially of those that believe."

1 Timothy 4:10

Chapter 1

Blake Gibbons picked himself up off the floor, where he'd been rolling around with a pair of dogs named Bruce and Wayne. The black lab licked his face and Blake chuckled. "You ready for me, Tess?"

A blonde-haired woman gestured him into the kitchen, setting the broom she'd been wielding against the counter. "Sit right there."

He took the stool his boss and the foreman at Brush Creek Horse Ranch had sat on. Then Tess and Walker's two boys. And now Blake.

"What do you want this time?"

"Shave it off." Blake didn't even reach up to touch his thinning hair. Only twenty-seven and already with a heinous receding hairline.

Tess's fingers swooped through his hair. "You sure?"

Blake nodded, his mind made up. "Yep. Take it off. I don't even care if you use an attachment."

"It doesn't look that bad if we keep it short."

"Yes, it does." Blake was tired of trying to make his hair

cover the balding areas. "I look like I'm trying too hard. I'm going bald. Might as well embrace it." Who he was trying to impress, and why, he wasn't sure. Just another reason to shave his head completely.

Tess switched on the clippers, the hum filling the air between them. "This isn't going to get it smooth," she said over the buzz. "You'll have to use a razor for that."

"I'm fine with a super short buzz."

"You'll look very military."

"I wear a cowboy hat almost all the time."

Tess smiled and started on his right side, just above his ear. "Yes, you men and your love affair with cowboy hats."

"They're practical," Blake said as Walker came back into the kitchen, freshly showered. His new haircut made him seem even more distinguished than he already looked. "Takin' it all off, huh?" he asked before opening the fridge and pulling out a plastic container. He popped the lid and the scent of dill wafted into the air.

"It's time," Blake said as Walker got down a box of crackers. They were headed into the summer months, and Blake didn't want to spend time he didn't have taking care of hair he didn't have. This haircut was a win-win in his mind.

Tess finished and used quick, short movements with the brush to flick the tiny hairs away. "There you go, cowboy." She unpinned the drape and starting oiling the clippers.

"Thank you, ma'am." He'd been getting his hair done by Tess since he moved to Brush Creek, almost three years ago. When she'd married Walker and moved up to the ranch, Blake had cut a half an hour from his schedule.

He reached for the broom and swept up his hair with a

single pang of sadness. He wasn't going to dwell on the loss of his hair. It was just hair.

Still, he knew women fantasized about a man's hair, and the loss of his almost felt like a death sentence. With every swipe of the broom, Blake told himself it didn't matter. He wasn't dating. He'd tried, but Brush Creek didn't have a lot of selection as far as potential partners went. The few women he'd gone out with had helped him learn that he wasn't over Jessica yet. Jessica, his high school girlfriend he'd longed to reunite with.

Jessica, who'd gotten married and moved to California over a year ago.

Blake bent and swept the hair into a dustpan, wishing he could swish away his negative thoughts just as easily.

"Any chance of me taking Wayne tonight?" he asked Walker.

Walker rolled his eyes. "You and that dog."

"He loves me." The black lab trotted over as if he'd try to get Walker's permission with his big doe-eyes.

"He likes to sleep on the bed with you and that mutt of yours." Walker held out the box of crackers, but Blake waved him away.

"The girls will be here any minute," Tess said, Blake's cue to get the heck out of there. Walker's too, judging by the way he leapt to his feet.

"Is that tonight?"

"Sure is." Tess gave him an affectionate pat on the shoulder. "Don't tell me you didn't know. I told you about it this morning. And last night. And the night before that."

"No, I knew." Walker met Blake's eyes and his expression clearly said he hadn't known.

"You and the boys want to come hang at my cabin?" Blake asked. "You can come if Bruce and Wayne come."

Walker chuckled and reached for his cowboy hat hanging on the peg by the backdoor. "As soon as you open that door, Wayne will run off. You know that, right?"

"He always comes back." Blake grinned, threw the hair clippings in the trash, and washed his hands in the kitchen sink.

Tess pulled out the tallest chocolate cake Blake had ever seen and set it on the counter. "I'll get the boys." She left the kitchen and called down the hall. A few seconds later, two tween boys—one dark like Walker and one light like Tess—appeared.

"My cabin, boys," Blake said, lifting his arm and slinging it over Michael's shoulders.

"Tess, will you save me some cake?" the boy asked his step-mother.

She grinned and giggled. "I made you guys your own cake. Remember I said you could eat cake for breakfast on the last day of school?"

Graham, Tess's biological son, whooped and they ran out the back door with the dogs. Walker followed them, but Blake headed for the front door, as he'd stopped here on his way home and his truck sat out in the lane.

He opened the door and stepped out—and right into a soft body. A woman cried out, and Blake tried to reach for her, tried to grab her. His fingers scrambled over hers, and he looked into a pair of stricken brown eyes before she fell down.

He'd just knocked down a woman. "I'm so sorry," he

said, his voice filled with embarrassment. He bent down and looked at her. "Are you okay?"

She forced a laugh through her throat and allowed him to take her hand and help her stand. "I'm fine." Her voice sounded with a decidedly sexy Southern twang, and Blake's heart drummed out an extra beat—something it hadn't done in a while.

"I really am sorry. I didn't know you'd be there."

She tucked her shoulder-length brown hair behind her ear and straightened her blouse. Blake peered at her, finding her unfamiliar. "I don't know you. I'm Blake Gibbons."

"Erin Shields." She held out her hand for him to shake. "I'm a friend of Tess's and I just moved to town."

He shook her hand, wanting to hold on a lot longer than necessary. "Oh yeah? What brings you to Brush Creek?"

"My aunt owns the pie shop here, and she needed some help. I said I'd come."

He checked her left hand for a wedding ring, but it was nearly dark and he couldn't tell for sure in the split second he allowed himself to look. "That's great," he said. The dating pool in Brush Creek had just gotten a new, beautiful, intriguing fish.

"Yeah, I guess." Erin shifted her feet, and Blake realized he was blocking her way into the house. "Tess is a better cook than me. I keep telling her she should help Shirley at the bakery."

"But then I'd be too exhausted to have chocolate nights." Tess joined them on the porch and gave her friend a hug. The look of happiness in her smile as she hugged Tess made Blake grin too.

"You made it." Tess linked her arm through Erin's and stepped around Blake to enter the house. He stood there dumbly, staring at Erin. She glanced back at him too, and dang if his blood didn't start on fire.

Then the door closed between them, startling Blake and reminding him that cowboys weren't invited to Tess's chocolate nights.

Chapter 2

Erin promptly forgot about the tall, wiry, blond cowboy the moment Renee showed up. Before that, though, she managed to ask Tess one question: "Who was that?"

Tess glanced at the door she'd just closed and said, "Blake?"

Erin shrugged one shoulder, glad the weather had started to warm up now that it was almost June. Tonight, she wore a blouse that left her shoulders bare but a sleeve that went past her elbow. Her bobbed hair swung a little with the movement.

Before Tess could say anything more—and she clearly wanted to if the interest in her eyes meant anything—Renee burst into the house. "There better be six different kinds of chocolate here tonight. Baby has a craving." She grinned like she'd won the lottery.

Erin laughed with Tess, then snapped her fingers. "I left my dessert in the car. Be right back." She hurried out to her sedan, the only one in the driveway. The other women who attended these shindigs lived at the ranch, and Erin took a deep breath of the mountain air, relishing her freedom. Immediately, guilt made her stomach flip. She loved her three children. She'd do anything for them. But sometimes, she was glad they went to Salt Lake City every other weekend to see their father. Glad she got forty-eight hours to herself. Sometimes she didn't do anything but lay around and watch TV, maybe indulge with a meal she didn't have to make or clean up after.

She grabbed the chocolate fruit tart she'd made at her aunt's house that morning. Aunt Shirley had been teaching her a few tricks and tips with pie dough and tart shells and doughnuts. Erin didn't seem to be very good at making crust light and flaky, or getting bread dough to rise properly, or figuring out how to get the oil hot enough before frying the doughnuts.

Looking at the beautiful tart, she thought she might get some bonus points for appearance. But as soon as her friends tasted the crust, her chances at winning that night's tasting would be lost. She'd known there was something wrong with it the moment she pulled it from the oven, but she hadn't had time to fix it.

Aunt Shirley had said she needed more butter, and her water should've been colder, and the oven hotter. How she knew that, Erin didn't know.

She re-entered the house and slid her tart onto the counter.

"Erin," Tess said, admiring the tart. "You made that?"

"Why do you sound so surprised?"

"I don't see any chocolate on that," Renee said, eyeing it dubiously.

"I brushed the tart shell with dark chocolate," Erin said. "Strawberries, raspberries, and blueberries, and chocolate."

Renee's expression turned to acceptance. "Oh, well, can't wait to taste it."

"What did you bring?" Erin asked.

"Molten lava cake." She gestured to the oven, where a delicious-looking cake sat, delicately sprinkled with powdered sugar.

Erin's mouth watered, at least until Tess said, "Erin was asking about Blake."

"No, I wasn't," Erin said automatically. She didn't want this girl gossip. She'd only said something to Tess because they were old friends, both of their husbands having worked together at the scrap metal yard Tess's first husband had owned.

But Renee had already seized onto the simple sentence. "Blake? Our Blake?"

Erin prayed for the ground to open up and swallow her. Or maybe Renee. "So, why are you craving six different kinds of chocolate today?"

Renee didn't seem to notice the topic change, because she said, "Do I need a reason when I'm pregnant?"

"No, you don't," Tess said with a laugh. "Almost out of the first trimester now. How are you feeling?"

Relief spread through Erin, and she caught Tess's eye. Understanding passed between them, and Erin knew Tess wouldn't bring up Blake again. At least not until they were alone.

Erin woke the next morning at three a.m. She groaned as she pulled herself from the warmth of her bed and went to brush her teeth. Half an hour later, she descended the steps from her second-story apartment to the bakery below. Shirley had already arrived, and she had flour up to her elbows.

She hummed as she kneaded, and Erin wished she was a morning person like her aunt. "Morning," she said with a yawn. Erin reached for the black apron hanging on the wall and tied it around her waist. "Am I on cookies again today?"

"Yes, dear." Shirley flashed her a smile and continued kneading.

Erin could make cookies. She was slowly learning the other things, but her aunt still didn't quite trust Erin to take over the bigger items like pies and tarts. That was the goal, as Shirley's husband had been recently diagnosed with prostate cancer and she wanted to be home with him more.

The bell rang out front and a moment later, Doug arrived in the back. "Morning, ladies."

Another morning person. Erin lifted her hand in greeting as she set the huge bowl in the mixer stand. Doug owned and operated the bakery half of the store, offering breads and rolls, doughnuts and cookies, cupcakes and birthday cakes. He had more business than he could handle, and his mother had been doing the cookies and doughnuts, along with her pies and fruit tarts, for a couple of years.

The goal was for Doug and Erin to partner on the shop, with Erin eventually taking over all Shirley did with the pie shop while helping with whatever Doug needed as well. Now, if Erin could do more than make a decent batch of chocolate chip cookies, the plan would be foolproof.

She slopped flour down the front of her apron as she attempted to weigh it and tried not to look up to see if Shirley or Doug had seen her blunder. She felt like a fish out of water, flopping around, trying to figure out how to survive.

It was a good offer, one that would ensure Erin had a way to provide for her children long-term. She'd been praying for something that would give her the freedom to be available for her children while still having the money she needed.

So when her aunt had called, Erin had jumped at the offer. Packed up her family in Vernal and moved them almost an hour northwest to the tiny town of Brush Creek she used to love to visit as a child.

Over the course of the next three hours, she made four varieties of cookies—double chocolate chip, cranberry and white chocolate macadamia nut, oatmeal raisin, and snickerdoodle—stocked the trays and set up the front of the bakery, and finally she switched out her dirty apron for a clean one before she unlocked the front door.

A line of about a dozen people waited, and she welcomed them with her warmest smile though she felt bone-tired already. Staying at Tess's until eleven was a huge mistake. She boxed doughnuts and bagged cookies and wrapped loaves of bread for about a half an hour before she caught up to the line.

With a moment to breathe, she restocked the trays, glancing up when the bell twinkled again. Her breath caught in her throat at the sight of the tall cowboy who entered. He swiped off his hat, and she recognized Blake Gibbons, who'd already run her over the previous evening.

"Hey." He smiled easily, his eyes singular on hers. "I didn't realize you actually worked here."

Her heart pattered irregularly, a fact which surprised her. With three children ages eight and under, with a year-old divorce, Erin didn't hold any hope that she'd find a new husband anytime soon.

Blake was handsome, that was all. He had a soothing voice. Muscles everywhere. Erin tore her eyes away and focused on the display cases in front of her. "Yeah, I'm helping everywhere I can for now." She cleared her voice, unsure of how much he knew about her uncle's health. "What can I get for you?"

He scanned the cases and said, "I'll take half a dozen glazed doughnuts and half a dozen maple bars."

Erin started boxing up his order. Before she finished, Doug entered the shop from the bakery in the back. "Blake," he said. "You want to come on back?"

Erin met his eyes, and something hot and charged passed between them. She ducked her head, sure she'd somehow entered an alternate universe where she actually thought a man would be interested in her.

Blake was likely several years younger than her, had never been married, and would change everything he thought about her—if he thought anything at all—as soon as he discovered she had three children.

She pressed herself into the display case as he passed behind her and slipped into the bakery with Doug. Despite the scent of yeast and sugar hanging in the air, she still managed to catch a whiff of his masculine cologne before he disappeared.

She finished boxing his doughnuts and set them to the side of the register for when he returned, her mind revolving around what Doug needed Blake for in the bakery.

Chapter 3

Blake took in the water damage in the back corner of the bakery, his brain only firing on one cylinder because of the woman in the front of the shop. As soon as he'd met her last night, he'd wanted to find a way to see her again.

And there she was, the first person he'd seen that morning. Half his brain whirred trying to find a way to see her again before he left the bakery, and the other half processing the amount of work it would take to fix the shop.

"This looks pretty bad," he said to Doug. He pressed two fingers against the wall, and it moved. Definitely not good. "How long do you think it's been leaking?"

Doug sighed. "All winter, probably. The foundation's shifted." He hung back as if the entire corner of the building would collapse on him if he got too close. "Can you fix it?"

"Yeah, of course." Blake glanced up, left, and right. "Can I see it from the outside?"

"Sure." Doug led him out the back door of the shop,

and sure enough, the structural and foundational damage was clearly visible from the outside.

"What's on the second floor?" Blake asked.

"Erin just moved in up there."

Blake's heart tripped over a beat before returning to normal. A smile slipped across his mouth, and he quickly straightened it. "It'll take a lot of work," Blake said. "And it won't be cheap." He glanced at Doug, whose shoulders stiffened.

"Define 'cheap'."

Blake crouched and examined the damage. "This will need to be rebuilt. Matched up with the other foundation. It'll be probably fifteen or twenty thousand dollars."

Doug sucked in a breath, and regret sliced through Blake. He wanted to help his friend, but his time and expertise was worth something. Not to mention supplies, trips to Vernal to get those supplies, and paying inspectors to approve habitation of the building.

"How long will it take?"

"Months," Blake said. "Probably all summer, since it's peak season on the ranch too."

"When's planting?"

"Next weekend, so I wouldn't be able to start until the week after that." Blake was already tired, thinking about all that needed to be done to prepare for planting, and then maintaining all the fields, and then mending sprinkling systems, managing the water rights. He barely kept up with all of that, and then it was time to harvest. Blake was in charge of all of the farming at Brush Creek Horse Ranch, and while the other cowboys spent their days training horses, he spent his making sure all of the animals on the ranch could eat.

"Let's do it," Doug said. "Did you bring the paperwork?"

Blake pulled out his phone and opened a note. "I didn't bring it. I need to take some measurements and some pictures. Then I'll draw it all up and bring it down for you to sign." His mind seized onto this as a way for him to see Erin again. Plus, if he had to be down here in the evenings after his work on the ranch concluded, maybe he'd get to see her then too. He couldn't erase the smile playing with his lips, even when he felt the weight of Doug's stare on his face.

He finished his note, and opened his camera. "I'll be in and out for a few minutes. All right?" He glanced at Doug, who nodded, wiped his hands on his apron, and went back into the shop.

Blake busied himself with snapping photos and making a few more notes. He went into the shop and repeated the process with the damage inside. He found Doug and asked, "Can I get into the apartment upstairs?"

"Let me talk to Erin." He finished swishing blue stripes of frosting across a tray of chocolate-dipped doughnuts and stepped through the doorway leading to the sales floor. Blake followed him, intending to get his measuring tape from his truck. He kept himself from so much as glancing at the pretty brunette as he left through the front of the shop. She was busy with customers anyway; even Doug waited to speak with her.

Blake grabbed the tape measure and went around the back of the building without going through it. He started at the corner and took the measurements he needed, stepping inside to do the same. The notes on his phone got longer and longer until he finally finished.

One of those glazed doughnuts and a cup of coffee from the drive-in down the street sounded heavenly about now. He turned when Doug said, "She can take you up, Blake."

Blake grinned at her and waited for her to move. He'd been friends with Doug for three years—since he moved to Brush Creek. He had a wicked sweet tooth, after all. But Doug had never lived above the bakery, and Blake had never been upstairs.

Erin moved around the preparation area and stepped through a door. Blake followed her, heat rising to his face. He hadn't felt this level of attraction for a woman since... well, ever. He'd been so hung up on Jessica for the past ten years.

Immediate foolishness flooded him. He'd grown up next door to Jessica, and he'd been in love with her for as long as he could remember. He'd left Colorado when she got engaged, hoping for a fresh start. But Brush Creek had excellent WiFi, and he'd been able to keep up with everything Jessica and her fiancé did online, including their fancy wedding at one of Colorado's premier ranches.

He thought once she tied the knot, he'd be free. He'd tried. He'd gone out with several women here in Brush Creek. As he reached the top of the stairs, he knew he'd never met anyone that had intrigued him quite as fast as Erin had.

She entered her apartment without unlocking the door

and stepped back to let him follow her. "What do you need to look at?"

"There's some foundational damage downstairs," he said, trying to keep his voice even. He scanned the apartment and found it in various stages of unpacking. Empty boxes had been flattened and stacked against the wall near the door. The apartment was one large room with a couch that faced a TV, a dining table behind that, and the kitchen in the far corner. Right where the damage was.

He groaned. "Notice anything leaking in your kitchen?" He stepped through the disarray, noticing children's sized shoes. A pang of alarm radiated through him.

"No," she said. "But we just moved in."

"You and your family?" He bent and opened the cabinet in the corner. It held a lazy Susan that hadn't had anything stacked in it yet. A musty smell hit him, and Blake's stomach dropped again.

"Me and my kids," she said.

Blake straightened, so many things happening in his mind he couldn't keep them all straight. "How many kids?"

"Three."

He blinked, once for each child, before asking, "Boys or girls?"

"Two boys, one girl." Erin glanced over her shoulder. "Did you find what you need?"

He glanced back at the cabinets. At the very least, she'd be getting a new kitchen. "This is worst-case scenario," he said. "Will you tell Doug I need to see him?"

Erin nodded and ducked out of the apartment. Blake realized too late that he could've gone back down to talk to Doug himself. He didn't need to send Erin away to do it. At the same time, he didn't need to be so obvious in his attraction.

Doug arrived a minute later, glancing around like black mold would be creeping up the walls. "What?"

Blake gestured to the cabinets. "It's behind all of this."

Doug scrubbed his floury hands through his hair, leaving streaks of white behind. "Will she have to move out?"

"Probably not. But she'll have to live in a remodel for at least, oh, I don't know. Let's say three weeks." The thought of spending three weeks' worth of evenings with Erin made Blake giddy. At the same time, a warning siren blared in his mind. She had *three* kids.

"How much?" Doug asked.

Blake cocked his head to the side as if considering. "What's Erin's story?" he asked instead of giving a quote. He'd draw that up in the paperwork anyway.

"Erin's my cousin. My father's ill, and my mom thought it would be nice to give her—" Doug stopped as if someone had pushed mute on his vocal chords. "Wait a second. Why are you askin' about Erin?"

Blake shrugged. "No reason. She's new in town. Did she grow up here?"

"No, in Vernal. Her mom is my mom's sister. They spent a lot of time together, so Erin did come here a lot, especially in the summer."

Blake nodded. Erin had come back to somewhere safe after something traumatic in her life. Blake was going to ask Doug if she was married, but now he didn't need to. She wasn't. She wouldn't need a job in the family bakery if she still had a husband.

"Want to go fishing this week? The spring runoff is still strong." Blake fiddled with his phone so he wouldn't have to meet Doug's eyes. He didn't want his friend to see his interest in Erin's life. Didn't need that getting back to her.

"Sure," Doug said. "Which evening?"

"Thursday is probably going to be best," Blake said, mentally running through his to-do list for the week.

"Thursday it is. I'll come up to your cabin."

Blake took out his tape measure and finished the job before heading downstairs. His doughnuts waited by the register, and he stepped up to purchase them, his mind racing. How could he see Erin again without being obvious? Where were her kids right now? How available would she be?

She smiled at him and tapped on the computer screen. "That'll be thirteen nineteen."

He handed her his debit card and she ran it. His mind blanked. This was it. He wouldn't see Erin again for at least a week. For some reason, his heart shriveled at the very thought.

"Am I really going to get a new kitchen upstairs?" she asked.

"There's been some water damage to the building."

"And you're going to fix it?"

"Yes, ma'am." He tapped the brim of his cowboy hat. "I'm a general contractor."

She handed his debit card back to him and waited for the receipt to print. "You look like a cowboy to me." Her cheeks turned rosy, and Blake wondered if she was flirting with him.

"That I am, ma'am." He signed the receipt she

presented. "I grew up on a huge farm in Colorado. My dad trained champion barrel racing horses for the rodeo circuit. My twin brother still rides bulls, and my younger sister is on the leaderboards in the W-PRCA."

"Did you do the rodeo?"

A flash of disappointment cut through him, though it had been years and he'd come to terms with his life. "I couldn't. I was really sick when I was a teenager, and I had a bone condition for a few years that prevented me from riding and training." He swallowed. "I would've loved to be in the rodeo, but I did what I could and that was farming. My dad taught me everything I needed to know to have my own farm or to manage one. That's what I do at Brush Creek."

"And the general contracting?"

"I went to school for that," he said. "Most farmers need a side business, and it helps to be handy so you can fix your own outbuildings on a ranch." He leaned against the counter, nowhere near ready to leave.

The bell sounded, indicating someone else had entered the bakery. He straightened. "Well, it was nice talkin' to you, ma'am." He picked up his box of doughnuts and started to turn.

"Do you go to church, Blake?"

He turned back to her. "Sometimes," he said, when he really should say "Hardly ever." Everyone up at the ranch were regulars at the little red brick building where the pastor spoke on Sunday mornings. Blake had gone a couple of times over the years, but he also enjoyed a day at the ranch by himself.

"Will you be there tomorrow?"

Deciding to be brave, he leaned in again. "Depends. Will you?"

Their eyes met, and Blake found the heated interest in her gaze. Saw her freckles pop out as a flush stained her cheeks. "My kids are in Salt Lake City with their father, so yes, I'll be there by myself."

"Well, I guess I better be there too, then." He tapped his hat again, turned, and left the bakery.

Chapter 4

Erin's heart didn't settle back into the right spot in her chest until several minutes after Blake left. When she woke the following morning, the organ had once again taken up residence in her throat.

She had no idea why she'd asked if Blake would be at church that day, only that she didn't want to sit by herself. Without her children, Erin didn't quite know how to be herself. In Vernal, she still had friends who'd never moved, neighbors who'd lived next door to her family, and her parents she could attend church with. Here, she had Aunt Shirley and Uncle Johnny, but with her uncle's declining health, she couldn't count on them to attend.

And she wasn't sure she could walk into the chapel alone, an outsider in this town she'd always loved but didn't quite fit into.

"Should've called Tess," she muttered to herself as she headed down the stairs and turned west toward the church at the end of the block. Cars and trucks passed her, and some patrons walked the path she did. She took a deep breath and entered the building behind a couple with two small children, probably close to her three-year-old McKenzie's age. A smile drifted across her lips as she followed them into the chapel.

She paused, stepping out of the way of another family when she realized she'd stopped right in the middle of the aisle. "Sorry," she murmured, every instinct inside begging her to leave, and leave now.

Erin turned and ran into a solid chest. "Oh—"

"Whoa there," a familiar voice said. A steady hand landed on her shoulder while another one wrapped around her waist, keeping her from falling down. Again.

"Blake."

"We've got to stop running into each other." He chuckled, his vibrant blue eyes intoxicating as he gazed down at her. He couldn't seem to look away, and Erin didn't want him to. "Have you found a seat?" Blake glanced around, the teensiest bit of apprehension on his face.

"No. Anywhere is fine." Erin shifted and Blake dropped his hands from her body.

"Well, how about this back row?"

"Nope," another cowboy said, stepping in front of Blake. "April and I always sit in the back." He carried a baby that looked close to six months old to Erin and waited until a tall brunette sat before he joined her on the pew. "You can sit on the other end, if you want." The other cowboy scanned Blake from head to toe. Then Erin. "If you came more often, you'd have a regular seat."

Blake sucked in a breath and guided Erin back into the lobby and into the other side of the chapel. He moved into the pew first and sat down, his neck turning a ruddy shade of red.

"You don't come to church that often, do you?" Erin asked as she sat next to him and straightened her skirt.

"Not that often, no." He sat straight and tall, his eyes straight forward.

"I don't do a whole lot without my kids," Erin said. Where the words came from, she wasn't sure. But she felt comfortable with Blake, and she wanted him to feel comfortable with her too. "I was nervous to come by myself." She cut him a quick glance. "I could've called Tess."

He tilted his head and met her eyes. "I don't want you to call Tess." He faced the front again, and she didn't know a person could sit so still, so straight. Surely his back would ache after only a few minutes.

But ten minutes later, the service began and Blake still hadn't moved. The silence between them wasn't the comfortable kind, and Erin wasn't sure how to fix it. She'd been hoping for a new life here in Brush Creek, one without awkward silences and difficult conversations and restless nights.

But nothing had changed just because the town had a different name. Helpless and frustrated, Erin wiped her eyes, which had begun to fill with tears.

"I'm sorry," Blake whispered as the preacher started to stand. "I should've told you I don't get down to church that often."

"It's fine," Erin whispered back. "It's not that."

Blake twisted and looked fully at her. He reached out

and swiped his thumb across her cheek. "Want to get out of here and talk about what it is?"

She didn't need more than a second to think about it. She nodded, stood, and left the chapel as quickly as her heels would allow.

SHE FOUND herself on a swing in the park, Blake next to her. They drifted lazily back and forth, the chains squealing with the movement. Her heels lay discarded on the edge of the playground, and a near-summer breeze played with her hair.

"My kids will be back tonight," she finally said. "They have two weeks of school left, and then they'll go back to Salt Lake for half of the summer."

Blake swung forward and back, forward and back. "Do you miss them when they're gone?"

"Yes."

"Tell me about them."

She looked at him, sure he didn't want to spend his time listening to her blab on and on about her kids. He tossed her a half a smile and his eyes shone with kindness.

So she started talking. "Cole is eight and he's about to finish third grade." A smile formed on her face and her heart lifted. "Davy is six, and he's almost done with first grade. McKenzie is only three, and that's why I live above the bakery. I have to get up really early, and if we live there, I can let the kids sleep while I prep and get the shop open. Then I go back upstairs and get them off to school, and McKenzie and I work in the bakery until lunchtime." She sighed and looked into the distance, where a man had just arrived with his dog and a Frisbee. He tossed the toy and the dog streaked after it.

"In Vernal, I taught the kids piano in the afternoons. But I couldn't bring my piano here." She wasn't sure why she'd brought that up, only that it had popped into her mind.

"My boss is an excellent pianist," Blake said. "I bet you could come up to his place and use his piano."

Erin scoffed and laughed. "Right. I'm going to drive up the canyon and borrow your boss's piano."

Blake chuckled too. "Yeah, probably not."

"So why don't you make it down to church very often?"

"Oh, so we're going there." He didn't seem angry, but the awkwardness between them flared back to life.

"You said we could talk if we didn't go to church."

"All right." He swallowed and twisted his chains toward her. "I'm not a super religious guy. Didn't really go growing up, and it's nice to be out at the ranch when everyone else is gone. It's…peaceful."

"Confession time?"

"Sure."

"I feel the same way when my kids are gone." She allowed herself to giggle. "It's a little hectic when they're here and it's just me trying to make sure no one dies."

Blake's eyebrows rose. "Does that happen a lot? The dying?"

Erin tipped her head back and laughed. "Not yet, no." She grinned at him, and he grinned back, and this time the silence felt…nice.

Erin's week passed in a blur of wake up, make cookies, serve customers, deal with children, clean up the bakery, take a quick nap, get kids from school, make dinner, deal with fighting in a tiny apartment, get everyone to bed, try to breathe.

By Friday, she was ready to ship them off to Salt Lake, the last week of school or not. The warm weather didn't help, as all Cole and Davy wanted to do was run around town, causing havoc. Not that they really could, and Erin did end up sending them across the stream, which ran behind the bakery, to the park.

Friday evening, she loaded the children into the car and headed for her aunt's house on the other side of the park. "Come on," she told the boys. "I have to work tonight. You're sleeping here, with Aunt Shirley."

Davy cheered, but Cole pouted. "Oh, come on," Erin said, cuffing him on the head, sending his brown hair flopping a little. "Aunt Shirley used to make the most delicious breakfasts when I slept here as a little girl."

"What'd she make?" Cole asked.

"Ebelskivers," Erin said. She'd tried making them once when the boys were little, but she'd failed spectacularly, just like she still couldn't make a pie crust that was acceptable to sell to someone else. Aunt Shirley acted like she didn't know, but the ruse that Erin could actually take over the pie shop was beginning to wear thin.

Desperation surged up her throat. She needed this arrangement to work out. Not only to help her aunt and uncle, but because she didn't have any other employable skills. She'd met her husband Jeremy her junior year of college, and they'd gotten married a year later, with Cole coming ten months after that. Erin hadn't finished college and had never had a job that provided her with her any skills she could use to make money.

Now, if someone needed a diaper changed or the hard water stains scrubbed out of their tub, she could do that. She knocked on Aunt Shirley's door, her thoughts spinning about starting a cleaning service in town.

"Hello?" she called, entering the house. Not much had changed since she was a little girl and had come to visit her mother's sister. The carpet had been updated, but the walls were still ecru, with the same pictures hanging on them. Brown brick made up the fireplace, and Uncle Johnny sat in a recliner—the same olive green one he'd had when Erin was a child—an oxygen mask over his nose and mouth.

He pulled it off when he saw her, a smile cementing into place. "Hey, who have we got here?" He rose from the chair, a wince of pain crossing his face. He didn't let it slow him down as he swooped across the room and plucked Mckenzie from Erin's arms.

"Who is this little princess?" He tickled the girl, and she giggled.

"It's me, Uncle Johnny," she said. "McKenzie."

"Oh, of course it is." He grinned at her and gestured for the boys to go with him. "I got the tent set up in the backyard. Come see."

"Tent?" Cole said, his eyes suddenly alive.

Erin followed them, leaning in the doorway as the boys burst into the backyard, whooping about the big blue tent not far from the patio. Warmth filled Erin, and she was glad she had family here.

"Erin, how are you?"

She turned toward her aunt, who had just stepped behind her. "Good, Aunt Shirley. Uncle Johnny set up the tent, huh?"

"Took him almost an hour." Aunt Shirley shook her head, a quiet laugh escaping her lips. "But he insisted."

Erin patted her aunt's arm. "I'll get their sleeping bags from the car." She stepped toward the front door. "Oh, and I may have mentioned the ebelskivers to Cole."

"Well, you better run to the market and get me some buttermilk then," Aunt Shirley said. "And probably some butter."

The last thing Erin wanted to do was an errand at the grocery store, because she also needed to make twelve dozen potato rolls that night for a mid-morning pickup the following morning. She retrieved the sleeping bags and pillows and tossed them in the tent. She grabbed Cole long enough to give him a quick squeeze.

Davy threw himself into her arms and said, "This is so awesome, Mom. Thanks," before running off, his arms outstretched like the wings of an airplane.

"Kenz." She took the girl from Uncle Johnny and kissed her forehead. "You be good for Aunt Shirley and Uncle Johnny, okay? Promise me and cross your heart."

The beautiful towheaded girl crisscrossed her heart and smiled before throwing her arms around Erin's neck. Her heart cracked a little at having to leave them here. In the eight years since she'd become a mother, she hadn't had to rely on anyone quite so much as she was now. It was a lot harder than she'd thought.

Once, she'd thought women who got to leave their children in someone else's care while they went to work were lucky. They at least got to have an adult conversation during the day. They could escape the endless and mindless chores of changing diapers and making sandwiches without the crust. But as she walked away, leaving her three babies behind, she realized that those women had just as many difficulties as she did. Maybe more.

She cleared her throat and straightened herself in the driver's seat. A quick trip to the market, then to the bakery. She could do this. She could do anything for a few hours. She could do anything for a few hours that would benefit her children.

―――

SATURDAY MORNING, she loaded rolls into brown paper sacks two dozen at a time. Monica Murphy took two bags, and Erin loaded herself up with a couple as well. She followed Monica to the door, her shoulders aching from all the kneading the previous night.

Doug had been in the kitchen in the back when she'd arrived, but he hadn't started. He oversaw, instructed, as she mixed, kneaded, formed, and baked dough. Thankfully, he'd proclaimed her work good enough, and they'd gotten out of the bakery by ten o'clock. It still wasn't early enough for her to get the rest she needed so she could be back by three-thirty to begin that Saturday's baked goods.

But she'd made it through the rush, and the rolls were

headed out, and with only a couple of hours until she could shower and take a nap, Erin renewed her resolve to finish strong.

With Monica satisfied and sure her family party would be a success, Erin returned to the bakery. "Blake," she said, one hand lifting to her throat.

He turned from the display cases, a smile dancing across his strong jaw. "Mornin', ma'am."

She shouldn't be so charmed by his manners, his cowboy twang, but she was. He made her feel a decade younger than she was. She gave him a cocked eyebrow. "It's hardly morning."

"I've been up since five." He yawned. "So I hear you. Feels like midnight."

She smiled fully then. "Right. Someone as young as you can go for hours."

"As young as me?" He leaned against the display case and held her gaze. "How old do you think I am?"

"Twenty-five?" she guessed.

"Close."

"Higher or lower?"

"Higher."

No way he was thirty. She aimed right in the middle. "Twenty-seven."

"Nice. Only two guesses." He studied her, and her face heated under the weight of his gaze. "So let me guess your age."

"You get two guesses."

"Hmm." His eyes narrowed as he considered her. "You have an eight-year-old, but you're also gorgeous, so you probably got married young."

Gorgeous rang through her mind like someone had struck a gong with the word imprinted on it.

"Thirty?" he asked.

She suddenly didn't want him to guess again, but she said, "Older," anyway.

He cocked his head, and in that dark gray cowboy hat, he became downright dangerous to her health. The bell rang on the door, and he turned at the same time she lifted her eyes to see who had come in.

A man Erin didn't recognize, probably close to her age. Probably married with a family, just like almost everyone else in this town. "I'll be right with you," she said. She looked back at Blake. "Are you going to buy anything?"

"Of course," he said. "Why else would I be down here?" His eyes twinkled like blue-diamond stars—they definitely said he'd come for another reason. "Let's see...." He scanned the cases. "We're planting this weekend, and we have a dozen extra cowhands at the ranch. They all seem to gobble up the sweets. I need five dozen of your square glazed doughnuts." His eyes came back to hers, hooked, held. "Do you have that many?"

Erin thought she could dive into his eyes and never resurface. "Let me check in the back." She walked away on wooden legs, her emotions spiraling tight and then releasing. She wiped the back of her hand across her forehead and forced a deep drag of air into her lungs. She really needed to stop finding Blake Gibbons so attractive.

Why, though? her mind whispered.

Cole, Davy, and McKenzie, the thought came right back.

She had more than enough doughnuts and she stuck

her head around the corner. "I've got them. You want them all boxed?"

"Yes, and I want an apple fritter in a bag."

She nodded and started filling the boxes. She rang him out and loaded up his arms with the five boxes, but he didn't turn and go.

"What are you doing tonight?" he asked.

"I have the kids."

"So you'll be home?"

"Most likely." She didn't have a lot of money for entertainment, and Oxbow Park provided more fun than anything else she could think of.

"Do you have a key to the bakery?"

"Yes." She really had no idea where he was going with all this.

"I might need you to let me in." He glanced at the man still examining the goods in the cases. "I'm going to start on the repairs in the back."

"Oh, sure." Foolishness snaked through Erin. Of course he wouldn't be making another fifteen-minute drive down the canyon just to see her.

"Great, thanks, ma'am." Blake's hand twitched to tip his hat and he almost dumped all five dozen doughnuts on the ground.

He flushed and Erin laughed as he walked out. She admired the gentle strength he emanated before turning to the next customer. "What can I help you with?"

Chapter 5

Every muscle in Blake's shoulders and back screamed at him to get into a hot shower as soon as possible. Then ice packs and Icy Hot, as much as possible for as long as he could stand it. Oh, how he hated the spring planting.

And it wasn't even finished yet. Thankfully, he had enough work to do all day tomorrow to keep him from attending church. The extra help Landon had brought in would stick around until the planting was done, but that was okay. Blake could handle a few extra guys for one day.

Two of those guys were staying with him, one in the extra bedroom and one in the loft, so by the time Blake's turn came for the shower, most of the hot water was gone. He scrubbed quickly and downed some painkillers.

"Megan's got pizza at the homestead," he said, donning his cowboy hat. "You guys can head over at six-thirty."

"You're not coming?" Gene, a cowboy from the cattle ranch on the south side of Vernal, asked.

"I have some business in town." Blake headed out the door, his heart tangoing in his chest the whole way to the bakery. He didn't have Erin's number, so he couldn't text her to find out if she was home, if she could let him in. He could call Doug, but he didn't want to see Doug.

Erin sat on the curb outside the bakery, a little girl by her side. The child licked an ice cream cone while Erin twisted toward her, a smile on her face and words coming from her mouth. She glanced over when Blake parked in front of the shop next door.

She'd stood by the time he got out of the truck, and she had the girl balanced on her hip. Her eyes broadcast her fear, and Blake approached slowly. "Hey, there." The little girl looked at him, and licked licked licked.

"What flavor is that?"

"Twist," she said, like that was a flavor.

Blake grinned. "Looks good. You must be McKenzie."

She snuggled into her mom's collarbone, the ice cream cone coming dangerously close to Erin's blue blouse. The color made her hair darker and her eyes more mysterious. Blake liked it, liked everything about her.

"Bakery's open," she said. "I was just waiting for my boys to come back from the park."

"What's happening after the park?" he asked.

"Dinner," she said.

He smiled, stepped past her, and went into the bakery. Ideas foamed in his mind, and while he pulled down damp and moldy sheetrock, he plotted ways he could get himself invited to dinner.

As the work progressed, his plans got dashed. No woman wanted a man showing up on her doorstep sweaty, covered in mold and mud. He hauled the ruined walls to the Dumpster on the side of the building and swept everything in the back corner. If he could get the exterior dry enough, it wouldn't have to be replaced.

He traced the crack that ran through the foundation with his fingertip, and he pulled out his phone to make a note about renting a Bobcat before washing up in the industrial-sized sink. He was about to sneak out and get over to the diner for a plate of chicken fried steak—the Saturday night special—when Erin appeared in the doorway that led upstairs to her apartment.

"Have you eaten yet?"

"I—I have other plans." She didn't need to know what they were.

"Oh yeah?" She stepped into the kitchen and leaned her hip against the counter that supported the sink. "And here I thought you'd come to see me." She gave him a knowing look, and Blake couldn't deny it. Didn't even want to.

"I've been contracted to work on the bakery." Doug had signed the papers Thursday night before their fishing trip.

"On Saturday night? After a full day of planting?"

"It's not going to fix itself, ma'am." He unclipped his tool belt and laid it over his toolbox.

"So you don't want to come upstairs for the most spectacular spaghetti dinner Brush Creek has to offer." Her voice sounded the littlest bit squeaky.

"I didn't say I didn't want to."

"Right. Other plans." Hurt passed through her dark eyes. Hurt Blake never wanted her to feel.

"I'm a little nervous," he admitted.

"Of what?"

"Your kids."

Her face blanked and drained of color. "What does that mean?"

"Oh, come on." He took a step toward her. "There's... something going on here. Right?" His throat suddenly felt like sandpaper. Surely he wasn't the only one who felt the river of electricity flowing between them. "I'm just nervous. I've never dated a woman with three kids."

Her eyebrows shot toward her hairline, and Blake took that as his signal to shut up, and fast. But he heard himself say, "Not that we're dating. I mean—I don't even have your phone number, and—" He pressed his eyes closed at the same time he managed to seal his lips.

He breathed in through his nose and out through his mouth. When he opened his eyes, Erin watched him with those glittery, black-coffee-colored eyes, a satisfied smile riding her mouth. Blake's mind blanked as he stared at her lips.

"Do you have your phone?" she asked, breaking his trance. He licked his lips, thinking about what it would be like to kiss Erin. His heart raced and she stood a good five paces from him. Still, something soft and floral teased his nose. A scent uniquely Erin.

"Yeah," he said weakly, pulling it from his back pocket. "Why?"

She closed the distance between them and plucked it from his fingers. She tapped and tapped, her thumbs flying across the screen. With a glint in her expression that ignited flames in his bloodstream, she handed the device back. "Now you have my number."

He glanced down at the phone. In the few seconds it took for her words and actions to register, she'd returned to the doorway and gone through it.

"Did you say spaghetti?" he asked.

"Sure did." She didn't pause or come back.

He lunged for the doorway. "One of my favorites. Am I still invited?"

"If you want," she said, her voice cool and detached.

Blake took a few extra seconds to think things through, but he didn't get very far. Erin was climbing the stairs, soon to open her apartment door and disappear inside. And he couldn't let that happen.

He took the steps two at a time and caught her with her hand curled around the doorknob. "Wait," he said, panting and every organ in his body doing some sort of bouncy dance. "What are you going to tell them?"

"Tell who?"

"Your kids." He gestured between the two of them. "I mean, what are we?"

"Friends?" Erin tipped up onto her toes, and for one terrifyingly wonderful moment, Blake thought she'd kiss him. Her eyes seemed glued to his mouth, and the desire was right there for anyone to see. He wondered how long it had been since she'd kissed someone. Wondered if she'd dated other men after her divorce.

"Can we be friends?" she asked.

"For tonight," Blake said, withdrawing his hand and enjoying the color as it rushed into Erin's cheeks. She twisted the doorknob and entered the apartment. Blake went with her, because he wanted to be where she was.

He was less than prepared for the chaos three children

could bring to a small space. Sure, he'd grown up with two siblings; his mother had dealt with three children under the age of three at one point. But they lived in a sprawling homestead on five hundred acres of land in western Colorado.

This apartment was the exact opposite of that. The noise was the first thing Blake noticed, and he admired the door for holding it in so expertly. The two boys chased each other around the couch. Around and around, the older one laughing like a super villain while the younger one screamed at him to "Give it back!"

McKenzie sat on the floor almost in the warpath of the boys, coloring. Every other stroke, her crayon left the paper and marked the floor. Erin stepped through it and grabbed something from the older boy. "You guys stop it. We have a guest." She nodded toward Blake, who stood at the door like a statue.

The younger boy took the recovered item and turned toward Blake, the altercation with his brother clearly forgotten already.

"You must be Davy," Blake said, the tremor in his voice entirely too real. He swallowed it. "And you must be Cole. Your mom's told me about you."

Davy bounded over to him and grinned. "Do you like Star Wars or Star Trek?"

"Uh...neither?" Blake looked at Erin with apprehension.

"Wrong answer," Erin said.

"How can you not like Star Wars?" Davy asked, incredulous, like Blake was the first person he'd met to say he disliked Star Wars.

"Cole, come help me set the table," Erin said from the kitchen. "Davy, get the Clorox wipes and clean up McKenzie's marks. Kenz, time to wash up for dinner."

Blake watched the family as it moved into motion. The children obeyed their mother for the most part—she had to tell Cole twice to put out the napkins—and he marveled at how all the cogs came together to create something beautiful. In this case, family dinner.

"Are you a cowboy?" Cole asked when Blake sat next to him at the table.

"Yes, sir. I work up at Brush Creek Horse Farm. That's where I met your mom." He flashed her a quick grin. "She got in my way and I ran right into her."

"Knocked me down and everything." Erin grinned and extended her hands to her kids. "Let's pray before we eat. Davy, your turn."

Blake awkwardly slipped his hand into McKenzie's and Cole's, both of which felt strange. One sticky—McKenzie's—and one too warm. Davy asked for good health. He gave gratitude for this apartment, the bakery, and Uncle Johnny and Aunt Shirley. He prayed that his dad would be safe, and that his mom would learn how to bake.

Blake almost laughed out loud at that one, but he kept the sound inside. The way the boy prayed for his parents, for their lives, touched Blake's heart. By the time he said, "Amen," Blake automatically added his ending to the prayer too.

He met Erin's eyes and let the laughter out. "You don't know how to bake?"

She lifted her chin and reached for a pair of tongs. "I should've said grace myself."

Blake laughed again, the sound freeing and feeling fantastic as it left his throat. Beside him, Cole squabbled with Davy about how he'd taken the spaghetti with all the meatballs. McKenzie started crying because her breadstick touched her noodles. Erin spent the next several minutes breaking up fights and calming the children. She hadn't even dished herself anything to eat by the time Blake finished his first plate.

His stomach revolted; his nerves felt like someone had gassed them and lit them on fire; his eardrums physically hurt. He had no idea what to do to help Erin. Even though he'd only known her for a week, he could see her getting more and more frustrated.

"That's it," she said. "No dessert if you don't all be quiet and eat."

That got them to settle down. They ate, but Davy didn't seem to know where his mouth was and he had more spaghetti sauce on his face than Blake thought possible. McKenzie slurped the noodles, sauce flying when the tail of each noodle got sucked into her mouth.

Cole glanced at Blake, who had no idea what to say. He finally landed on, "Do you like fishing?"

The boy looked at his mother, who nodded. "I've never been."

"You've never been fishing?"

"Yes, you went last summer with Grandpa."

"He didn't even let me touch the pole," Cole said.

Blake looked at Erin. "Tell me this isn't true."

"Not everyone shares your affinity for catching fish." She rolled her eyes. "Plus, Jeremy—" Her eyes widened, and she seemed to have difficulty swallowing. "My ex-husband worked a lot. He didn't take the kids to do things."

"And you're anti-fishing, is that it?" Blake tried to tame the teasing quality of his voice, but the kids didn't seem to notice he was flirting with their mom.

"Not anti," she said. "Just...disinterested."

He looked back at Cole. "Well, maybe when school gets out, I can take you fishing."

"We're going to Salt Lake forever," Davy said.

"Not forever," Cole said. "It just feels like it."

Blake leaned back in his chair, the conversation taking a turn he didn't know how to deal with.

"You guys have fun at your dad's," Erin said with a measure of coolness in her tone.

"But not for six weeks," Cole complained. "We finally move out of Gramma and Grandpa's basement, and now we—"

"Cole," Erin warned.

"I want to stay here," he continued anyway. "Davy does too. We can go to the park, and go fishing, and set up the tent in Uncle Johnny's yard."

"You can do that when you get back in July."

Blake listened and volleyed his gaze back and forth between Cole and Erin. Neither seemed happy. This conversation wasn't new either. Blake absorbed details he didn't know yet, like that she'd lived with her parents in Vernal.

"Mom—"

"Cole," she said sternly. "Drop it now."

He glared at her, and she stared right back. A shiver traveled down Blake's spine. He wouldn't want Erin looking at him like that. In fact, he'd do anything she wanted just to get her smile back.

"Can I be excused?" Cole asked through tight teeth.

"No, you're on dish duty tonight."

"I did dishes last night," he complained.

"Wrong," she said. "You guys slept at Aunt Shirley's last night, and I know she ordered pizza."

McKenzie reached for something—what, Blake didn't know—and knocked over her water glass. She immediately started crying, allowing Cole to mutter something under his breath and Davy to jump back from the table as the water gushed toward him. His chair clattered to the floor and chaos ensued.

As Blake sat there, he felt one-hundred percent overwhelmed. Senses on overload. Patience already gone.

How Erin did this every day of her life was a complete mystery to him. He'd been sitting there for thirty minutes and he needed a dark, silent room to recover. Fast.

By the time he managed to get out of there without seeming rude, a headache had been throbbing behind his eyes for ten minutes. He sat in his truck and looked at the lit square windows of the apartment above the bakery.

"You're in way over your head," he said to himself. He could end this right now. He'd done nothing but blunder a few words about dating. He hadn't kissed the woman. Hadn't made plans to see her again.

Even if he liked Erin, he was in no position to become a father to three kids. He'd persuaded himself for the last week that he could take things slow, find out why she'd gotten divorced, meet the kids and start to get to know them.

But he felt like he'd just been thrown to a pod of hungry sharks, with a wound that was gushing blood. And he'd only eaten a plate of spaghetti with three kids.

He leaned his head back and sighed, everything all a jumbled mess in his mind. He liked Erin, but he wasn't sure he was ready for everything she brought with her.

Chapter 6

Erin let her tears fall once she got the children to bed. Spaghetti and meatballs waited in the kitchen, along with a special kind of mess that only three children could produce. She methodically put the leftovers in plastic containers, stuck them in the fridge. She picked up shoes, sweatshirts, and backpacks.

She unpacked two boxes and put the contents in the front hall closet, the kitchen, and the linen closet outside the bathroom.

She scrubbed the table, the counter, everything she could wipe down. She swept, the swish-swish of the broom good background noise for her weeping.

She wept because she was sure she'd just lost any chance she might've had with Blake. She shouldn't have invited him to dinner so soon. He needed to be much more involved with her before she let him see what family life was like. At least her family life.

The boys had been especially obnoxious today, and she

could no longer deny how unhappy Cole was when he went to Salt Lake to visit his father. He'd been complaining for a few months that their dad was never home, that he never took them to do anything, that he hired a babysitter who didn't know how to cook.

He'd said they had to stay inside the house all the time, that all they did was watch TV, that he didn't even have a bed to sleep in. When Erin had asked Jeremy about the bed situation, he'd said he was "Working on it."

Her sadness weighed so much, and it felt like a yoke around her neck. With the apartment finally clean and somewhat organized, she rubbed the back of her neck, trying to ease the tightness there. She sank onto the couch and closed her eyes.

I blew it, didn't I? she thought. Lord, help me know what to do about Blake.

She didn't know what to do about him, and the next time she opened her eyes, it was because McKenzie had said her name and touched her face. Weak morning sunlight filtered in through the blinds as she gathered the little girl into her lap.

"What are you doing up, hummingbird?"

"I went potty," the little girl said.

Erin stroked her daughter's feather-soft hair and listened to her breathe. "Should we make pancakes for breakfast?" Erin didn't want to get off the couch, but she knew if Kenz was up, the boys wouldn't be far behind. Might as well get them sugared up before she had to take them to church.

Properly mapled and carbed, Erin got the kids settled in

the back row where she and Blake had sat last week. For a brief moment, she watched the entryway, half hoping he'd show up and help her with the kids during the sermon.

She'd given him her phone number, but he hadn't used it yet so she didn't have his. She sat on the end of the bench to keep the kids boxed in, and tried to find a single second of solace while her children were behaving.

The pastor got up and smiled out to the crowd. He had the kind of face that could endear people to him in moments, and Erin found herself enthralled by him. He started speaking about living a good life, something Erin had been trying to do. Sometimes life felt really heavy to her, though, and she wasn't sure she could lift the weight by herself. As the preacher spoke, she realized she didn't have to. She could give her burdens to the Lord.

Her phone buzzed, distracting her from her epiphany. She glanced at her lap and found an unknown number. Her first instinct was to ignore the text, but something caught her eye.

Even if you can't bake, you make great spaghetti and meatballs.

A grin jumped onto her face, but she had no idea how to respond to Blake's text.

Can we talk? Maybe later tonight?

And she certainly didn't know how to answer that. *We need to talk* was never good, and besides, she'd seen the way he looked last night at dinner. Like he was witnessing a zombie apocalypse. He'd practically run from her place, citing some lame excuse about needing to get back to feed his dog. She didn't even know if he owned a dog.

She didn't like how she doubted him, didn't like feeling

knotted up inside. She flipped her phone over and refocused on the pastor. She needed this reprieve, and she could easily cite church as the reason why she couldn't text back right away.

AN HOUR BEFORE EVENING, Erin tucked her keys in her jacket pocket and reached for the Mississippi mud pie she'd spent most of the afternoon creating. "Kids! Let's go." She'd called Tess and asked for an emergency chocolate meeting, just the two of them, and her skin felt like she'd injected red ants just under the surface.

"Davy, help Kenz with her shoes. I'm going to take this pie down to the car and I'll be right back." By the time she had everyone in the car, sweat had formed along her forehead. She practically collapsed into the driver's seat and turned down the radio that one of the kids had cranked up.

"Mom," Cole whined, reaching for the volume knob again.

"Cole," she said back, turning the sound down again. "It's too loud. I can't think."

He folded his arms and pouted, sending a shockwave of guilt through Erin. She tried to ignore him, but ever since the divorce, she'd found herself giving in and allowing her children whatever they wanted just to make them happy.

It hadn't been easy for any of them to leave their schools, their friends, their father, and moving three hours away. They hadn't had their own house but had lived in her parents' basement, and that hadn't been easy on anyone.

And now she'd brought them to Brush Creek, to a small apartment over a busy bakery.

They still want to be here rather than with Jeremy, she thought as she navigated through town and found the road that led up to the ranch. She'd rather be here than with Jeremy too. She'd loved Brush Creek as a child. The town held a magical quality; the sunshine healed; the people were kind and accepting.

Please help Cole when he goes to his father's next week, she prayed, glancing at her son again. *Please help Jeremy understand how to give them a good experience.*

She often prayed for that knowledge herself, and she had no idea what she was doing most of the time. She knew her children needed food, a place to sleep, and hugs. She did all those things. But she didn't know how to help Cole deal with his feelings, or how to help him understand that his dad loved him but had some priorities that compromised his ability to show it.

Erin shook her head. She would be forever tied to Jeremy, but he didn't get to dictate how she lived her life anymore. He'd stopped being able to influence her when he decided his job was more important than his family. When his wandering eye kept him from coming home at night.

Gravel crunched under her tires as she gained the top of the hill. The horse ranch spread out before her, and Erin marveled at the mini community this place was. The only other time she'd been here, she'd been so focused on finding Tess's house that she hadn't paused to soak in the beautiful landscape here, the well-kept homestead, cabins, and grounds.

In front of her, a man led a horse across the lane from

the side where all the ranch outbuildings stood to the side where the cabins lined the white-gravel road. He didn't go toward one of the cabins, and Erin could tell from the man's gait that it wasn't Blake. He'd said he didn't work with the animals, so she shouldn't have expected it to be.

She pulled to the left and parked half on the grass and half on the road in front of Tess's house. "All right, guys," she said. "Let's be on our best behavior, okay?"

No one answered her as they all piled out of the car. She retrieved the Mississippi mud pie from the trunk and walked across the lawn toward the front door. It opened before she arrived, and Tess came out onto the porch. She leaned against the pillar as two boys followed. They were older than Cole, but his face lit up anyway.

"Cole," Erin said as they approached. "These are Tess's boys, Graham and Michael."

"Last time I saw you," Tess said. "You were a tiny baby." She drew Cole into a hug and released him with a warm smile. "The boys are takin' the dogs down to the creek."

"Can I go?" Davy asked, and Erin beamed at him as she nodded.

The four boys ran around the cabin, and several moments later, a big black lab appeared at the corner of the house. A boy called to him, and he tore back the way he came.

Erin laughed as she shook her head and handed Tess the mud pie. "I come bearing chocolate."

"Oh, boy." Tess looked at the pie and then Erin. "That bad, huh?"

Erin looked at McKenzie, who rarely left her side these days. Tess set the pie on the kitchen counter and knelt down in front of Kenz. "Do you want to watch a movie?"

Kenz bobbed her brown-haired head and tucked her chin to her chest. Tess scooped her up like she knew how to deal with a three-year-old, though Erin knew perfectly well that Graham had just turned ten years old.

But Tess took a giggling McKenzie into the living room and started climbing a ladder into a loft. "There are bean bags up here, and a little fridge with water." Tess set the girl down and a few minutes later she returned, the pingy sounds of a cartoon wafting down from the loft.

"She's all set." Tess tucked her hands in her back pockets and exhaled. "So, are we talking about Blake?"

Erin dropped her eyes to the pie and tossed her keys and cell on the counter next to it. "What do you know about Blake?"

"I know everything that happens on the ranch—my husband is the foreman. He knows everything, and he tells me."

"Everything? He tells you everything?"

Tess laughed, her super-short pixie haircut barely moving. "Fine, he doesn't tell me about the horses and stuff. But he did say Blake's been acting weird. Going down to the bakery all the time." Tess hipped Erin out of the way and opened a drawer to pull out a knife.

"Yeah, Doug's hired Blake to repair the shop. Apparently there's been some structural and water damage from last winter." Erin swiped her finger through the whipped cream on top of the pie.

"Sure," Tess said. "And Blake has a wicked sweet tooth."

Erin grinned. "That too. I think he's eaten about a dozen doughnuts this week alone."

"Mm hm. Are you sure that doesn't have anything to do with the woman making them?"

"You think he has a crush on Aunt Shirley?" Erin dissolved into giggles, the sheer fact that she was with Tess improving her mood drastically. And she hadn't even eaten any pie yet.

"Your aunt still isn't letting you do more than cookies?"

"No, I do the bread now too. Takes some of the burden off Doug."

"But nothing with the pies."

"Not yet."

"How does she expect to retire if she won't let you take over?"

Erin hadn't come up here to discuss her job frustrations. She had a job, and that was all that mattered. She shrugged. "It'll be a slow transition. Aunt Shirley just doesn't run the front of the house anymore, that's all. I think that itself helps a lot."

Tess sliced the pie and put three pieces on three plates. "Let me run this out to Walker." She stepped through the back door, but held it open with her hip. Walker sat on the stoop and said, "Thanks, love," before Tess turned around and let the door close between them.

"Didn't think you'd get married again," Erin said, her voice much too forced to be casual.

"It's strange, isn't it?" Tess glanced at the closed door. "We've both lost spouses, we were friends for years, ran this little cotton candy stand at the apricot festival." She half-laughed, half-sighed. "I can't have more kids, but we have our boys and the dogs." She gave a little shrug, but Erin could see that being unable to have more children hurt her friend. "We're happy."

"I'm glad," Erin said.

"What about you?"

Erin knew exactly what Tess was asking. "It's been... difficult. I moved in with my parents, but I couldn't stay there much longer. We'd already been there a year, and...." She let her voice trail into silence. "I haven't dated anyone since the divorce was final."

"How long's that been?"

"Thirteen months." Erin slid a bite of pie into her mouth and found it more bitter than sweet. No wonder her aunt wouldn't let her make the pies and tarts. She barely knew how to sweeten something. "But it was over before that. Before McKenzie, even. I thought if we had another child...." A sob choked her words and she shook her head as she regained her composure. She took another breath and though she didn't want to consume more of the pie, she shoved a very large bite into her mouth.

Tess let her have her time. Then she asked, "How are the children settling into school?"

"Fine. It's the end of the year. They missed the testing here. I only send them so they don't shred the apartment to bits." She tried for a smile. "They're going to Salt Lake for six weeks this next weekend. They'll be back just after the Fourth of July."

"And?"

"And nothing. We live here now. The boys have their bunk beds, in their own bedroom. Kenz sleeps with me still.

The apartment is small, but it's free, and I have a job. Jeremy pays his child support. I'm making things work."

"All right." Tess had only taken one bite of her pie and the rest of it sat untouched on the counter. "Well, let's just see why you texted *and* showed up with pie, then." Tess lunged for Erin's phone and danced away with it, a gleeful smile on her face.

Erin followed her into the living room and made a futile attempt to get the phone back. "Tess."

"Oh, see, he *does* have your number." She glanced up and quickly back down. "You make great spaghetti and meatballs," Tess read from the screen. "Can we talk?" She lowered the phone and met Erin's eye.

"Yeah, that's why I texted." She sank onto the couch.

Tess joined her, her blue eyes searching Erin's now as she handed the phone back. "Are you seeing him?"

"No. I mean, he comes into the bakery."

"What's with the spaghetti and meatballs?"

"He stayed for dinner last night after he finished ripping down the walls in the bakery kitchen." Erin felt very far away from herself, like she could see an image of herself but couldn't quite grasp what was going on around her.

"And Ted said he saw Blake with a, and I quote, 'a pretty little brunette' at church last week. Apparently the couple didn't stay for long. Was that you?"

Erin nodded. "We left and went to the park to talk. I—blast it, Tess, I think I like him." She looked up and everything inside her felt cut wide open, exposed, for everyone to see.

"Well, of course you like him. He's tall, and handsome, and a cowboy."

Erin rolled her eyes. "I was never the one who was a sucker for cowboys."

"Me either." Tess relaxed back into the couch. "I mean, until now, of course. I really like cowboys now."

"Good thing, since you're surrounded by them." Erin sighed happily, but her mood shifted quickly back to the reason she'd come up the canyon. "So, I haven't answered him yet. He wants to talk tonight." She checked her phone. "Which means I have about an hour to figure out what to say to him."

Chapter 7

Blake knew exactly how many minutes and hours had passed since he'd texted Erin. He also knew she'd seen the text, because his phone put a little "Read" next to it, which meant she'd tapped on it and opened the text.

He'd spent the afternoon rationalizing that he'd sent the text during church. Maybe she'd glimpsed it, but not read it. And she was alone with her children today. Maybe she'd taken a long afternoon nap because she got up in the middle of the night, baked and waited on customers for eight hours, and then dealt with her three kids by herself for another ten hours.

He'd spent the morning pacing. Then he'd texted Erin. Then he'd taken Rosco, his blue heeler mixed mutt, out to the fields. The dog liked to run, and Blake liked to be outside. His head cleared when there was nothing between him and the sky.

Today, he'd seen more clearly about Erin. He really liked the woman, considering how little time they'd spent together. He liked the soft yet fierce nature of her eyes. The lilt in her laugh. The strength she possessed, whether she knew it or not.

He kicked at the dirt road where he walked. "She has three kids, Blake. Be reasonable."

And reasonable, rational Blake knew he wasn't ready to be a father to an eight-year-old, a six-year-old, and a three-year-old. He was barely ready to be in a relationship with a woman.

His compulsion to check on Jessica and her new husband had been strong today—another reason Blake had escaped his cabin. He tipped his head back, almost losing his cowboy hat. He held it in place with one hand, his voice saying, "Lord...."

He didn't have anything else to say. He'd spoken true when he'd said he wasn't raised in a religious household. He'd gone to church in Brush Creek a handful of times, on days when he didn't want to be alone.

But the fact remained that Blake liked being alone. He liked the solitude of the ranch, the wide nature of the sky, the distance between him and the rest of the world.

"Just another reason to stay away from Erin," he said, glad he had this empty space where he could release his thoughts. Rosco came panting up beside him, a stick in his mouth. "Oh, what've you got there, boy? Huh?" He tried to grab the stick, but Rosco dodged and galloped up ahead of Blake.

He laughed and let his dog go, grateful for the four-legged companion. "I'm grateful," he said, seizing onto the feeling. He looked into the sky again. "Lord, I'm grateful... I'm grateful to be here at Brush Creek."

His prayer turned inward, silent inside his own mind. I'm grateful for Rosco. For Landon and Megan, who provide a job for me and a place where I can live.

His thoughts wandered to the rodeo he'd missed out on, but he pushed them away. He wanted to focus on what he did have, not what he didn't.

I'm grateful for Erin.

The words crossed his mind before he could truly think them. They lodged in his brain, wondering what he possibly had to be grateful for when it came to Erin. They weren't dating. He'd barely held her hand for longer than four seconds.

And yet, he was grateful for her introduction into his life. He wondered why she was there, what he was supposed to do with this well of attraction and his racing heart every time he thought of her.

His phone buzzed and chimed, and Blake whipped it out of his pocket. Relief rushed through him when he saw Erin's name. *I'm at Tess's house. I can leave my kids to play with hers if now's a good time to talk.*

His thumbs flew across the letters. *Now's great. I'm about ten minutes from my cabin. Want to meet there?*

Sure. Which one's yours?

Second to the end, opposite end from Walker and Tess's.

Great. See you in ten minutes.

Blake's throat tightened and dried out. He'd wanted to talk to Erin, but now he only had ten minutes to figure out what to say.

He'd barely stepped through the backdoor and filled Rosco's water bowl when someone knocked on the door. It wasn't Erin unless her hands had multiplied by ten. Sure enough, Walker poked his head into the cabin in the next moment.

"Blake?"

"Right here." He straightened, Rosco at his feet lapping up the water with slurping noises.

"I was sent to tell you that Erin will be a few more minutes." He stepped into the cabin and glanced around, something clearly on his mind.

Blake hadn't slept well the night before, and exhaustion kicked him in the chest. "How many more minutes?"

"They're women. I have no idea." Walker moved into the kitchen and sank onto a barstool. "So you and Erin Shields?"

"No, I don't think so. That's why we need to talk."

Walker didn't react, and Blake got out a couple of bottles of water from the fridge. "You thirsty?"

Walker reached for the bottle and twisted off the lid. "Why can't there be a you and Erin Shields?"

"Simple answer? I'm not ready."

Walker drank his water and patted Rosco on the head. "When's the last time you went out with someone when you thought you were ready?"

Blake opened his mouth to answer, but nothing came out. He'd dated Jessica in high school, but he hadn't been ready to be in a serious relationship then. He'd held onto her for so long that anyone else he'd gone out with had been on a surface level. He'd known it, and it hadn't taken the women he went to dinner with long to figure it out.

But Erin…. "Erin's different," Blake said, completely not answering Walker's question about his past love life. "She scares me."

Walker chuckled. "That's how you know you're ready." He clapped Blake on the shoulder and clomped out of the cabin. Blake stared straight ahead, his mind numb.

Lighter, more delicate knocking sounded on the door, startling him like gunshots. He jumped up from the counter and went to answer it, finding Erin in the pool of yellow light on his porch.

"Hey," she said, tucking her hair behind her ear in a gesture Blake found adorable. In a lot of ways, she was miles more mature than him, a dedicated mother of three. In some ways, he found her to be flirty and playful, like most of the single women he'd been out with in the past three years.

Without thinking, without second guessing, without a single word, Blake stepped forward, swept his arm around Erin's waist, and pressed his lips to hers.

He wasn't sure what he expected. The taste of chocolate flooded his mouth, and he drank in the soft smell of her skin. His pulse thundered when she kissed him back, knocked his cowboy hat to the ground as her fingertips flitted over his ears and along his scalp.

"You don't have much hair," she whispered against his lips.

He smiled, a rush of self-consciousness almost overcoming the euphoria of kissing a woman and meaning it, *feeling* it. "Shh," he said, molding his mouth to hers again.

―――

"HERE YOU GO." Blake draped a blanket around Erin's shoulders. After that kiss that had changed his entire perspective on life, they'd settled on his front stoop with their fingers entwined, the sun dipping closer and closer to the horizon.

When she'd shivered, he'd gone inside for a blanket.

"So are you going to talk?" she asked.

He swallowed, his bravery all dried up.

"I know my kids are crazy."

His fingers tightened on hers. "They're just kids." As he said the words, he realized the truthfulness of them. They were just kids. They did what kids do—and they'd been through some hard things in the past little while.

"I did get scared," he said.

"I saw it on your face." She glanced at him and nudged his chest with her shoulder. "Moms know everything, you know. You can't hide anything from us. We find out, eventually."

He growled and ducked his head so his mouth grazed her ear. "I don't want you to be my mother."

She pushed him back playfully. "Behave yourself."

He didn't want to, but he straightened and chuckled as he looked across the lane. The homestead sat down the road to his right, and his view went straight past the house to the horse arena beyond it.

"Blake, I...like you. I want to keep seeing you around the bakery, maybe up here at the ranch. But, I do have three kids, and." She turned toward him, and Blake looked straight into her beautiful eyes. "I'm interested, but I need to take things slow."

"Slow is fine, Erin."

"Is it?"

He spread his free hand toward the land before him. "I have nowhere else to go."

She snuggled into his chest.

"I have some questions," he said. She stiffened in his arms, but he pressed on. "I've been wondering why you got divorced. I mean, you obviously love your kids, and—"

"My ex-husband worked a lot," she interrupted. "Which was fine. He was—is—the foreman at a large scrap metal salvage yard in Salt Lake City." She took a deep breath. "It was the other places he'd go when he said he was at work that bothered me. I, uh." She cleared her throat. "Stayed for a while. Years, actually. Went to two different marriage counselors because he thought the first one was against him."

"All right," Blake said, his heart tearing a little at the betrayal and pain in her voice. He rubbed his hand along her upper arm. "All right, Erin." He didn't need to know more. He knew there were two sides to every story, and if he allowed himself to get caught up in Erin's life—which he'd already done—he would eventually have to deal with the ex-husband.

Blake shook his head, trying to dislodge the thoughts. He was thinking so far ahead, and he hated that. Didn't want to be kept up at night by his mind as it circled when he'd meet her ex-husband, how her kids would take the news of him dating their mom, any of it.

He just wanted to enjoy the sunset with her at his side.

"He stepped out on me six times," Erin said. "Six. Before I left."

Anger dove through him, along with the fierce need to protect her. "I'm sorry."

She breathed in deep. "I am happier here than I've been in a long time."

"That's good."

A dog barked, and Blake looked down the line of cabins to see Bruce and Wayne racing toward him, four boys chasing them with wild abandon. "Incoming," he warned Erin, who jumped to her feet as the slobbering hounds arrived.

Blake joined her, putting himself between her and the dogs. He scrubbed Wayne's head and said, "Rosco's inside, you big brute." He reached behind him and opened the door, letting the black lab inside. Rosco barked once, and the sound of claws scratching on hardwood met his ears as he pulled the door closed.

"This is Bruce," he said about the yellow lab. "He's about a hundred years old." The dog panted and collapsed at Blake's feet. "See? Harmless."

The boys arrived then, and Blake picked up Graham and swung him around. "Hey, bud," he said, laughing with the boy as he set him down. "Have you met Miss Erin?"

"Yes, sir."

"Hey, Blake," Davy said, panting, and Blake turned toward him.

Trepidation pulled through him. How could he know exactly what to say and do with Graham, but Davy made his brain go blank? "Davy."

The other boys arrived, and Michael gave Blake high five. Surprisingly, so did Cole. "Dad says we have to go to bed soon. School tomorrow."

"I think that's my cue." Erin put her arm around Davy. "Time to go, boys. Is Kenz still at the cabin?"

"She fell asleep," Cole said.

Erin yawned, and Blake mourned the fact that Walker and Tess had sent four witnesses to his goodbye. "See you later," he said to Erin as she looked at him.

"Will you be coming to work on the bakery tomorrow?"

"Maybe," he said, thinking through his schedule for the following day. "Might not be until the weekend."

"Until the weekend, then." She gave him a look that said she wished she could kiss him goodnight too, and sauntered into the darkness with the kids.

"Tell your dad I'm keeping Wayne for the night!" Blake called after Michael.

He turned around and walked backward. "He already knew you would." He laughed and spun back around to catch up with the rest of the group.

Blake chuckled and entered his cabin to the joyful, slobbery faces of Wayne and Rosco.

Chapter 8

School ended, and Erin packed up most of what the kids owned and drove them to her ex-husband's house. The house she used to share with him. She didn't go in but sat in the car on the curb and texted him that she had arrived.

An unfamiliar car sat in the driveway, and when Jeremy came out of the house, Erin caught sight of a woman. Her lungs iced, and she couldn't say anything. Not even goodbye to her children as they piled out of the car.

Jeremy strode across the lawn, seemingly happy to see them. He collected their bags from the trunk, and the echo of his voice came through the closed windows. Erin sat there through all of it, numb and cold.

Even after he'd ducked down and given her a thumbs up, after they'd all disappeared inside, and the bright red door which she'd painted herself one cold Valentine's Day six years ago had closed, she sat in the car.

The drive back to Brush Creek took a very long time.

At least it seemed that way to Erin. She may have cried at some point. Her face felt stretched tight and crusty when she showed up at the bakery. It was well past noon, so the parking lot was empty and she would be able to get upstairs without seeing anyone.

She pulled around the back of the building, almost smashing into a pickup truck already parked there. Though she'd only seen the truck a couple of times, she recognized it as Blake's. Her soul split. Part of her wanted to see Blake, tell him all about who she'd seen at Jeremy's, get his reassurances. Another part wanted to slip upstairs undetected, step into the shower, and find as much ice cream as possible. And a third part wanted to back onto the road and keep driving until she ran out of gas.

Several seconds went by while she made her decision. She got out of the car and went inside. She paused at the bottom of the stairs, and looked up. She could go straight up and lock the door behind her. Or she could walk into the kitchen, where a low radio played and a tenor voice sang along with it, missing about every third word.

A smile ghosted across her face, and she stepped into the kitchen. As she leaned into the doorframe, she said, "Hey, stranger."

Blake spun, the hope bright on his features. He grinned and strode toward her. She laughed as he caught her up in his strong arms and kissed her.

"Hey, yourself." He set her down and touched his forehead to hers. "You get the kids dropped off okay?"

She nodded, her words stuck behind the lump in her throat. She pressed her face into the hollow of his neck, inhaling the sexy scent of his skin. Aftershave and sweat and everything that got her pulse pounding.

"How long will you be here?" she asked.

"Well, I have the water turned off in the building, so I need to patch up everything around the pipes." He glanced over his shoulder toward the corner where he'd been working. "I need to put in the insulation and patch the sheetrock."

"Sounds like hours then."

He chuckled and drew his lips across her jaw. She trembled in his arms and gripped his shoulders as her strength flew from her. "Probably a couple of hours, yeah." He touched his lips to hers and pulled away.

"Are you saying I have no water in my apartment?" Her hopes of a hot shower grew dim in her mind.

"That's what I'm sayin', yeah." He covered her mouth with his this time, and kissed her properly. She sighed into him and released her worries. Her kids weren't here, would be gone for six full weeks. She could really get to know Blake Gibbons in that amount of time without risking any harm to the children.

As she lost herself to his heated touch, she knew she was only risking her heart.

THE FOLLOWING WEEKEND, she sucked in a breath and held it as she watched the timer she'd set for the six pie crusts she had in the oven. Aunt Shirley busied herself with tart pans, seemingly unconcerned, but the tension in the air was a palpable being.

The buzzer went off, and even though Erin had been staring at the timer, she still jumped. She snatched the towels off the counter and pulled open the oven. She searched the tins, her heart leaping against her breastbone.

"They look brown," she said. She reached for one, careful to not disturb the flaky pastry she'd so delicately pinched into a pattern along the edge. Erin slowly slid the tin onto the counter, the way she'd seen Aunt Shirley do. After she retrieved all six piecrusts, she beamed at them like they were her babies.

"They look beautiful," Aunt Shirley said. "In go the next ones."

Erin startled. "Right." She collected the next six piecrusts from the fridge and got them in the oven. She twisted the timer, an extraordinary sense of pride filling her. She hadn't felt like this in a long time. Everything in her life had been coming up as a failure for years, and while something as simple as a piecrust shouldn't make her so happy, those six, golden pastries brought her inexplicable joy.

"No time for staring. You've got fillings to make." Aunt Shirley laughed, and Erin joined in. She reached for the recipe for lemon curd, the first pie her aunt was trusting her with. Seemed like a lot of whisking.

"And these go on the cooling rack," Aunt Shirley said as she passed with a tray of tart shells. She stuck them in the bottom oven and helped Erin get the piecrusts where they belonged. Erin had no idea pastry could sweat, and she didn't want to ruin what she'd worked so hard to achieve.

Nothing could dampen her mood that day, and the hours selling doughnuts, rolls, bread, and cookies passed in a blink of an eye. She headed upstairs, where her routine had really started to get into her blood. Shower. Eat lunch. Take a nap. In the late afternoon, when she woke, she wandered through Oxbow Park behind her house. She'd found a footbridge about a half a block down from the bakery that led across the stream, and though she'd been visiting for a few days, the park was so large that she hadn't explored all of it yet.

She always returned to her apartment by five o'clock, hoping to see Blake, but he hadn't come all week. He'd been texting her, and she'd learned that he wasn't one for phone conversations. The one she'd tried to engage him in had gone poorly and lasted for only three minutes and twelve seconds.

She smiled just thinking about him. If he didn't come down to the bakery tonight, she was planning to get in her car and get herself up the canyon. The road went both ways, and if he was too busy or too tired to come work on the bakery, she thought she could sit...wherever it was he worked and keep him company.

When she woke from her siesta, her phone flashed. Blake had texted. *Dinner tonight? Let's get out of Brush Creek.*

Out of Brush Creek sounded wonderful, and she told him so. A meal she didn't have to make sounded like a little slice of heaven. She slipped into a red and black sundress only moments before Blake texted to say he was pulling in.

Her heart blipped. She grabbed her purse, ran her fingers through her hair, and skipped down the steps. Blake met her just outside the doorway. "Whoa," he said, adding a laugh. "Slow down, sweetheart. You're always tryin' to run me over." He slipped his hand into hers and let his gaze slide down her body. "Nice boots."

She lifted her heel and twisted her ankle to show off the red and brown cowgirl boots that matched her dress perfectly. "Thanks. I ordered them for my birthday."

"Your birthday?" His deep voice rumbled from his chest and into hers. "When's that?"

"Wednesday." She turned toward his truck and swung their hands as they walked in that direction.

"And I'm just hearing about it now?" He opened the door for her, his hand lingering on her waist as she climbed in. "You don't give a man much time to prepare."

She gazed at him, the slightest bit of dread coiling in her bloodstream. "You don't need to do anything."

He scoffed and leaned into the cab. "Right. Like I'm not going to do anything for my girlfriend's birthday." He chuckled and closed the door. She watched him round the front of the truck, muttering to himself.

Girlfriend rang through her head. She hadn't been anyone's girlfriend in a very long time. A decade. She rather liked the sound of it, especially from Blake.

"Seriously," she said when he got in. She slid across the seat and tucked her hand into his. "This dinner can count. I know how busy you are during the week."

"This dinner doesn't count." He gave her a disgruntled look and put the truck in reverse. "We're not eating tacos for a birthday dinner."

"I like tacos."

"Erin."

"What?"

"Why don't you want me to do anything for your birthday?"

She sighed. "It's just...I'm getting older now. I don't need fanfare."

"Rubbish," he said. "You made it through another year." He glanced at her and squeezed her hand. "And it was a hard year, don't try to deny it."

Emotion worked its way up her throat. It *had* been a hard year. She nodded as a tear splashed her cheek. She made to swipe it away quickly. "Dinner and a movie would be lovely. Sometime next week?"

"You want to come up to my cabin on Wednesday after you get done at the bakery?"

She faced him now. "I get off at noon."

"I work seven days a week," he said. "I can take half a day off. I have one of those hot air poppers...I'll make your popcorn as buttery as you'd like."

"Sounds wonderful."

"I'm not the greatest cook, but I can probably put something together. What do you like?"

"Hmm." She exhaled. "My mother used to make the best meatloaf ever. It had these little chunks of red peppers and this gravy...." Her mouth watered.

"Well, uh, I can't say I've ever made a meatloaf before."

Erin giggled. "You can just order pizza. I like double pepperoni."

"I'll surprise you."

She groaned. "I don't like surprises."

"Oh, be spontaneous." He turned into the parking lot of a Mexican restaurant. Erin hadn't realized they'd left

Brush Creek, but she did recognize the hottest restaurant spots in a neighboring town.

She twisted and pressed her lips to his, taking him by surprise. "How's this?" she asked, her mouth catching on the edge of his. "Spontaneous enough for you?"

He growled and kissed her back, leaving her breathless and giddy.

Chapter 9

Blake took the whole day off on Wednesday. He woke at dawn, as usual, and he didn't waste any time getting started on the cooking. He didn't do a lot of actual recipe-reading to feed himself. In fact, he popped two toaster waffles in the toaster and smeared peanut butter on them to make a waffle sandwich for breakfast.

Then he smoothed out the piece of paper where he'd written down Erin's mother's recipe for meatloaf. He worried that she might flip out when she found out he'd called her mother in Vernal to get the recipe, but he really wanted to make her birthday something special.

He read the whole thing again, got out all the ingredients, lined them up on the counter. He set the oven temperature and followed the directions to get the meatloaf mixed and in a bread pan he'd had to buy along with all the groceries.

Whistling and quite proud of himself, he slid the loaf pan into the oven. "Now for the gravy...."

By one o'clock—when Erin said she'd arrive—Blake felt like he'd prepared an entire Thanksgiving Day dinner. Meatloaf, mashed potatoes, green peas with lots of butter. Her mom claimed those were Erin's favorite. He'd asked her to bring a loaf of bread from the bakery, and he'd almost called Doug and ordered a cake.

"Here you go," Tess said, banging the front door open with her foot. "I'm so sorry I'm so late. I checked, and I don't see her car." She hurried into the cabin and set a three-tiered chocolate cake on his counter. She sighed and wiped the back of her hand across her forehead. "Wow, look at this. You made all this?" The pure shock in her eyes wasn't hard to find.

"I can read a recipe, Tess."

"There's a big difference between reading a recipe and actually cooking." She grinned. "Can I send Walker over here when it's my birthday?"

"Get out," Blake said with a smile.

Tess laughed. "You're welcome for the cake."

"Thanks for the cake," he called as she left.

He took stock of his preparations. The air popper sat on the counter by the stove, with a bag of kernels nearby. He'd called his mother to get her magic recipe for triple cheese popcorn. He'd found the cheddar cheese powder, Parmesan cheese, and buttermilk powder easily enough. But the nutritional yeast? He'd asked his mom if he really needed that, and she'd insisted he did. So he'd done what any good boyfriend would do: He marched himself across the street to the ranch owner's wife, and asked her.

Megan had promptly pulled some from her pantry, but at least a dozen questions rode in her eyes. And Megan was just like every other woman on this ranch—she found out everything. If she didn't know Blake was dating Erin Shields yet, she'd know by nightfall.

"Knock, knock." Erin stepped into the cabin wearing a pair of tight jeans and a blue blouse that revealed one entire shoulder.

Blake forgot his own name. "Happy birthday!" He spread his arms wide to indicate everything he'd prepared.

She paused and drank it all in before her eyes came back to his. "What is this?"

"Your mother's meatloaf." He pointed to the pan he'd put in the warm oven to reheat the meatloaf. "Mashed potatoes—with cheese. Buttered green peas. All your favorites. Oh, and the cake. But I didn't make the cake. Tess made the cake." Blake snapped his mouth closed and watched Erin closely.

Her chin wobbled and her eyes turned glassy. "Don't cry," he said. Though he suspected they were happy tears, he didn't know how to deal with them at all.

"This is wonderful," she said. "Thank you." She stepped into his arms and tipped her face back. She wore a smile as glorious as a summer sunrise.

"Happy birthday, beautiful." He kissed her, glad he could provide this one day of happiness for her.

WEEKS PASSED in a couple of blinks for Blake. He worked the fields, worked at the bakery, worked to find time to spend with Erin. When he went down to the bakery on Friday and Saturday evenings, he ended up falling asleep on her couch. He then saw her at church on Sunday mornings. He always brought her back to the ranch after church.

They'd eaten a few times with Megan and Landon. Sometimes he managed to put together something she would eat, and once, she'd brought the ingredients she needed to make smothered pork chops and asparagus.

Blake liked having Erin at his cabin. It felt natural to see her move around the kitchen, looking for silverware and a cutting board. Rosco seemed to like her just fine, even if she wasn't very fond of him.

"So the kids are coming home next Saturday, right?" he asked as they walked out of the church building together.

"Right."

"And have you decided if I get to go with you?"

She sighed and stopped right in the middle of the sidewalk. "I don't think it's a good idea."

"Why not?" He'd tried to understand how Erin felt, tried to put himself in her position and what he might do to protect his three children. But first and foremost, he wanted to support Erin, and he knew driving eight hours in one day would tax her. Seeing her kids after six weeks would likely make her emotional. "I want to be there with you."

"And I need to talk to my kids about us first." She started walking again.

Frustration drove him to continue. "Couldn't you just say you brought me along as a second driver?"

"Blake." She shot him an annoyed look. "I just don't think it's a good idea."

He stuffed his hands in his pockets. "Fine."

"Don't be mad."

"I'm not mad."

"You'll have plenty of time to get to know them." She wrapped her arms around him, but he remained still, unyielding. "Blake." She pouted, and Blake tilted his head to look down at her.

"Am I stupid if I say I'm scared?" he asked.

She fell back like he'd struck her, her mouth working but no sound coming out. "Of my kids?"

He focused on the brilliant blue sky around them. "Yes. Of you being someone different because they're back." He sighed, feeling like the most selfish man on the planet. Of course Erin would be someone different when her kids were back. She was their mother—and she acted like it. Without them, he'd started to fall for the flirty, fun woman who wore red cowboy boots and skin-tight jeans. Who held his hand whenever they went out. Who sat with him while he patched walls and tore out diseased bricks. Who kissed him like she was falling for him too.

And yes, he was afraid that woman would disappear. That all her guards would come flying back into place, that he'd have to fall in love with a different woman if he wanted to keep her in his life.

He realized she no longer stood in front of him but had continued down the sidewalk toward the bakery. She was almost to it now, and she didn't look back as she wrenched open the door and disappeared inside.

So it was happening already. Blake sighed and twisted back the way he'd come, squinting into the sunlight. The red brick church beckoned to him, and he had to admit he didn't mind the time he spent there. The preacher had a way with words, and Blake had felt safe and happy inside that building.

He faced the bakery again, and out of the two, he needed the peace and comfort of the church. So he headed back the way he'd come, a prayer entering his heart without a conscious thought from him.

BLAKE DIDN'T SEE Erin again until the following Friday, as had become their usual schedule. He'd texted her throughout the week—also their normal routine—and while she'd responded, he'd thought her answers were a bit shorter and definitely less enthusiastic than they had been previously.

He would be finishing the bottom corner of the bakery that night. The brickwork had been completed last week, and the foundation repair the month before that. Tonight, he'd be texturing the new sheetrock and painting the interior of the kitchen, making it match up with what already existed there.

The yellow bricks on the exterior of the building were brighter than the others, but he'd suggested to Doug that he rent a power washer and give the whole bakery a shine.

Nerves assaulted him on the drive down the canyon. His stomach hurt like he hadn't eaten in days, and he couldn't swallow the lump in his throat no matter how hard he tried.

In the past, Erin had been waiting for him in the kitchen, and he really wanted her to be there tonight too. Thankfully, she was. Sitting on the bottom step, flipping her phone over and over.

"Hey." He entered, not quite sure where they were in

their relationship. Suddenly, he didn't care. He set down his supplies and reached for her hand, pulling her to her feet. "It's so good to see you." He breathed her in and kissed her. "Leaving early tomorrow?"

"By seven." She clung to him, and he wondered if she'd miss the person she was without her children too.

"Erin." He smoothed her hair back from her face. "I'm sorry."

She smiled at him, a closed-mouth smile that touched his heart. "They're just kids, Blake. I've seen you with Tess's boys. You're so much more relaxed. You just need to be like that with Cole and Davy too."

"They did seem excited about fishing, didn't they?"

"I don't even see how that's possible, but if you took your dog, they'd probably like that." She danced away from him and boosted herself onto the stainless steel table where she sat to watch him work.

He chuckled and said, probably for the twentieth time, "Fishing is very relaxing."

Chapter 10

Erin's jaw hurt because she'd been clenching it so tightly for the past few hours. She had to get out of the car this time, as none of her children had phones and they'd need help with their bags.

On their weekend exchanges, Erin and Jeremy had met in a tiny town about an hour and a half from Vernal. Jeremy would usually get all the clothes and toiletries back, but she'd never sent her kids away for six weeks. She hoped they'd managed to get all their things.

She killed the ignition and strengthened her resolve before crossing the lawn to her old house. Memories surged forward, and she felt like throwing up. This was why she didn't want Blake to come. She didn't want him to see her in this vulnerable state, think less of her while she struggled to control the children.

She knocked, and it took several seconds for someone to open the door. When they did, she barely recognized Cole, his hair was so long. "Hey, bud." She wrapped her arms around him and laughed. "I've missed you."

He hugged her back but asked, "What are you doing here?"

She jumped back and stared at him. "You're coming back to Brush Creek today."

"We are?" He turned and yelled, "Dad! Mom's here."

At least Jeremy was home. *Not fair*, Erin told herself. She more than anyone should know that children didn't always tell the truth, and even if they thought they were right about something, the facts were very rarely facts.

"Erin?"

She came face-to-face with her once-husband, a tall man with dark, curly hair. Her chest seized, only because she didn't quite know how to be in the same room with him and breathe at the same time. She blinked, and flashes of her past life with Jeremy flowed through her mind. Happy times. Sad times. Devastation. Betrayal. Anger.

"What are you doing here?" he asked. "You're a week early."

She shook her head. "No. July tenth. Six weeks."

"No, I get a month and a half with them." He lifted the grill-sized spatula and gestured it toward the backyard. "We're barbequing today." He turned like he'd walk away from her, go back to his precious hamburgers.

"Jeremy, I need you to get them packed up."

He barely looked at her. "No. I get them for another week."

"No—"

"Erin, they're my children too." He rounded on her, anger flashing in his dark eyes. "Check the blasted court documents. I get them for a month and a half. Not six weeks." He glared at her for another moment before continuing into the backyard.

Erin spun away from him, hot tears pressing against the backs of her eyes. Cole stood there, worry all over his face. She smiled at him, though her vision blurred. "It'll be okay," she said. "I must've gotten the date wrong." She ran her hand along his hair and cupped his chin. "Where are your brother and sister? Maybe I'll just give them a hug before I go."

"In the backyard." He hurried through the living room and kitchen and followed his father outside. Erin felt so out of place in the home she used to keep. When Kenz and Davy burst into the house, the strangeness evaporated. She hugged them and smiled at them. She wanted to take them home with her so badly, but she didn't doubt Jeremy. In the end, she kissed her kids and made the lonely drive back to Brush Creek.

———

ONE WEEK and one day later, she had retrieved the children and gotten them and most of their belongings back to Brush Creek. She braided McKenzie's hair and called to Davy to find his church shoes.

Blake was meeting them in the chapel. She checked the clock hanging on the wall. He was probably already there, saving the back bench for when she finally got everyone ready.

"Let's go, guys." She grabbed her phone and lifted Kenz into her arms. Two steps out the door, she wished she had planned to drive. Even though it was only a block to the church, the July sun felt like fire next to her skin.

She was sweaty by the time she arrived in the chapel. "Blake saved us a seat," she said, her voice more aloof than normal. None of her children seemed to notice. She'd wanted to ask Cole about Jeremy, and if he had a new girlfriend, but she'd held her tongue. She'd learn everything about the month and a half her kids had spent in Salt Lake City sooner or later.

Entering the chapel last, and right as the preacher came down the aisle to begin, she handed McKenzie to Blake and hurried the boys onto the pew. "Sit down, sit down." She wasn't sure why she cared. No one sat behind them to complain.

She sat herself on the end, blocking all the kids in, and glanced down to Blake. He balanced McKenzie on one knee and was bent around her. He glanced down the row to Erin and smiled a smile that sent warmth through her soul.

He leaned over and said something to Davy, whose face lit up. He glanced at his mom and climbed over Cole to ask, "Can I go fishing with Blake?"

"When?" That question sent Davy scrambling back to Blake, so Erin held up her hand and pointed toward the pastor. Davy's face fell, but Blake tapped him on the shoulder and said something else to make him smile.

Watching them, Erin had the briefest burst of hope that they could find their way through all the obstacles so they could be together. She startled at the thought, because that meant she felt more for Blake than she'd meant to feel.

She snuck another look at him, knowing she'd started to fall in love with him.

Erin checked and double-checked the ground before stepping. Blake and the boys were way in front of her, and she'd used her three-year-old as an excuse for going so slow. She was just so unsure out here in the wilderness, with such uneven ground and no path.

Thankfully, Blake didn't have enough fishing poles for her to have her own. Why someone would own more than one fishing pole was beyond her. She'd said she could just supervise, maybe dip her feet in the stream, but she had no intention of taking her shoes off out here where there could be rusty nails or various piles of dung.

By the time she arrived at the stream, Blake had the tackle box open and two poles ready to go. Davy bounced around, he was so excited, and once Blake had the third pole done, he knelt down on one knee, her boys surrounding him. Even McKenzie wandered over to hear what he was saying.

She couldn't hear distinct words, but the timbre of his voice tickled her eardrums and made her smile. He demonstrated several things. Then he brought out the worms.

The excitement practically radiated off of Davy, and he baited his own hook and went to the edge of the stream just like Blake had shown him. Cole was a little bit more reluctant, but he managed to get his worm on the hook and cast the line into the water.

Blake did too, and Erin discreetly pulled out her phone. She snapped a photo of the three of them, their backs to the sun, their fishing poles in front of them. Blake stepped over to Cole and said something, adjusted his grip.

The afternoon faded into evening, with Erin sitting on a rock Blake called his "lucky fishing spot." She wasn't sure if she believed him, but he caught four fish in an hour, so perhaps he had spoken true.

With his catch done, he reeled in his line and helped the boys. Cole caught a fish first, and Erin hadn't seen that much happiness on his face in a long time. Her heart warmed even as the temperature cooled.

"Should we get back?" she finally asked when the sky turned orange and pink.

"Yeah." Blake sighed as he stood. "What a great afternoon." He grinned at her and slipped his fingers in hers for just a moment before stepping away to help with the fishing poles. They hadn't talked about appropriate behavior in front of her kids, but Blake seemed to know she didn't want to put on too much of a display in front of them.

By some miracle—and a steady stream of prayers—she made it back to solid, flat ground.

"Go on and put those poles in the shed," Blake told the boys, handing his to Cole. McKenzie had kept up with everyone this time, and she currently walked by the dog. Blake grabbed Erin's hand and tugged to get her to stop.

"Thanks for coming." He leaned in and kissed her. She fisted her fingers along his collar and kept him close even when he pulled back.

"Thanks for having us."

"You're not much for fishing." He gazed at her with soft eyes, no judgment in his tone.

"As long as I don't have to touch the worms, I like it fine." She stepped back and glanced toward the shed. The boys were still inside; Kenz still laughed up ahead.

She got everyone packed up and in the car, and they headed back down the canyon. "Did you guys have fun?"

Davy cheered and Kenz nodded, and Cole said, "Yeah, fishing was all right."

She took a deep breath. She wanted to talk to her children about Blake, and she figured while they were all trapped in the car was a great time. Then they—Cole really—couldn't get upset and run away.

"Do you guys like Blake?" She wasn't sure what she'd do if they didn't. She'd thought a lot about it in the month and a half the kids had been gone. Her kids had been through a lot, and for a few years there, she'd put Jeremy ahead of them. Which was fine. She knew a marriage required hard work, and she'd been married to him before any of the kids had come along. In theory, she'd be with him long after they left.

But not anymore, and now she needed to figure out what to do. Did the kids come before her own happiness? Could she date Blake—possibly marry him—if one of the children didn't like him?

She simply didn't have many answers.

When the kids all indicated that they liked Blake, she said, "I've been seeing him. You know, like dating. We're—we're dating." Her fingers tightened on the steering wheel and she glanced at Cole, who rode in the front seat of the car.

"Oh, that's okay," Davy said. "Dad's dating this lady named Jasmine. She's nice too. I mean, not nice like Blake, because she never took us fishing, but she's still nice."

Erin had a hard time swallowing, and she nearly ran off

the road because she kept her gaze on Cole for so long. He didn't say anything, and he didn't look at her.

"Is that okay with you, Cole?" she asked once Davy stopped talking.

He turned toward her and she saw something new in his eyes. She'd seen it at Jeremy's last weekend too, but she'd been so distressed she hadn't noticed. He'd matured. He saw things with different eyes now, and he shrugged. "I guess."

Without a guidebook for how to talk to her surly preteen about his mother dating a new man, she nodded. She'd take "I guess" for now.

Chapter 11

Blake thought the next several weeks went quite well. Everything on the ranch hummed along like normal. He'd moved upstairs in the bakery to assess the damage there. He felt bad that he'd had to rip out Erin's kitchen to get to the walls behind the appliances, but she did have ovens and whatnot downstairs.

Every time he asked her, she said she was managing just fine with her kitchen in shambles. On the weekends, while he worked in the apartment, Davy and McKenzie seemed enthralled by him. Davy asked an endless stream of questions about what he was doing, why did he need the fan to blow for three days, what was that blue stuff he put on the pipes, why did the windowsill need to be level. What even was level?

Blake liked the kid a lot, and he tried to answer every question. Erin often fed him those nights, and he'd stay like he used to when the kids were in Salt Lake. Finally, after she'd gotten them all to bed, he could kiss her and talk to her privately.

She'd told him she'd mentioned to the kids that they were dating, but he still felt uncomfortable kissing unless they were alone.

"They're down," she said one weekend before the apricot festival. She sank into the couch beside him, and he lifted his arm over her shoulders and cradled her against his chest. "I'm tired."

"It's been a long week," he agreed. In just a few short weeks, it would be harvest time, and he'd be pulling long hours to get her kitchen done before then. "I should be done on those walls tomorrow. Maybe next Friday. Then Doug will get the new appliances in, and I'll come back and paint everything up nice and new."

"Mm." Erin had closed her eyes, and Blake let his fall shut too.

"Have you talked with the kids about going to the apricot festival?"

"Yes. They're excited."

"So we're on for the festival next Saturday, the concert in the park that night, and the parade?" The town did a lot more than that during the week-long extravaganza, but that was all Blake could do.

"And Davy wants to do the fishing contest. Apparently they fill the stream here with hundreds of fish and the kids wade in and try to catch one. No pole necessary."

Blake nodded. "I've heard of that. I think Graham did it last year. It's for kids ten and under."

"Cole asked if Graham and Michael would be going to the festival." She twisted toward him. "Will they?"

"Yeah, Walker and Tess run a cotton candy booth to raise money for people who've lost spouses."

"Oh, that's right. Tess told me about that." She fell silent for a few minutes, and Blake thought she'd fallen asleep. His nerves teemed. He wanted to talk to her about a few things. Namely, how she thought things were going between them, because he felt like everything was going really well.

"Erin?" he asked.

She didn't answer; her chest rose and fell evenly; she'd fallen asleep.

"Erin, I think I'm in love with you," he whispered.

The apricot festival arrived, and the atmosphere at the park radiated fun and family atmosphere. Blake hadn't really enjoyed going in the past years, and as he walked down the path between the booths, he realized why. Everyone here belonged to someone else. Whole families, with generations of people, filled the open area at Oxbow Park. Someone like him—single, without attachments—didn't quite fit in.

He squeezed Erin's hand, feeling emotional today. She hadn't heard him tell her he loved her, and he'd spent the last week berating himself for the whispered words. He'd just meant to check in with her, see how she was feeling. She'd asked him to go slow, and to give her time. He owed it to her to do both.

So he'd made a pact with himself. He would not be saying any sentences with only three words. Not today. Not for a long time.

They wandered through the park, buying cheap jewelry,

and cotton candy, and fresh oranges. He bought everyone scones with raspberry butter, and later, when Erin said she was thirsty, he went and got lemonades and sodas.

She'd brought a couple of big blankets for them to sit on during the concert in the park, and no sooner had he returned and popped the top on McKenzie's soda did she spill it. All over the blanket.

"Up, up, up," Erin commanded, scrambling off the blanket before the soda seeped into her shorts. Blake complied quickly while Davy and Cole watched from the other blanket. Erin told McKenzie she needed to be more careful and they all piled onto one blanket.

"This is dumb," Cole said a few minutes later. "When are they going to start?"

"In a few minutes, bud," Blake said, thoroughly enjoying himself. No work. No worries. Clear blue sky. Beautiful woman at his side. A...family.

"Why can't I sit with Graham and Michael?" he asked for probably the tenth time.

Erin hissed out her displeasure and said, "I don't negotiate with terrorists. I said no. We're going to the concert as a family."

"Blake's not part of our family." He glared at Blake, who glanced away. "He's been hanging out with us all day."

"Not you," Erin said. "Remember how you ran off with Graham and Michael the moment we got here?" She gave him a dirty look. "And stop being rude."

Cole fell silent, but Blake's heart thundered in his chest. He thought he'd been getting along just fine with the boy. They played board games together on the weekend, and he'd taken Davy and Cole up to the ranch last Saturday while Erin worked in the bakery. They'd run with Rosco along the lane in front of the cabins until Graham and Michael had finished their chores, and Blake had watched all four boys for hours. He'd taken them for ice cream in the next town over. It had been a great day.

The concert didn't start in a few minutes, and Blake swallowed his discomfort. The heat started to annoy him, and then Davy and McKenzie started squabbling over the single bag of popcorn Erin had purchased.

Cole grabbed it, spilling half of it, and snapped at Davy. "Hey," Erin said. "Give it back."

Cole glared at her and slowly dipped his hand into the bag. "No."

Erin blinked, shock coloring her face a bright pink. "Cole, you chose the candied nuts. Give the popcorn back."

Davy made a swipe for it, but Cole held it out of reach. To spare Davy from launching himself at his brother, Blake said, "Go on, Cole. Do as your mother says."

"I don't have to do anything you say," he said, sneering at Blake. "You're not my father." He threw the bag of popcorn on the ground, spilling even more of it, and leapt to his feet. He stomped away while Blake stared after him, his chest so, so tight.

"Cole!" Erin called after him. She started to get up, but Blake put his hand on her shoulders.

"I'll get him." He went after the boy, easily keeping his eye on him as the crowd waited on blankets, making Cole the tallest moving target. The concert started just as Blake reached the back of the crowd, and disappointment lashed through him. He'd wanted to have a fun evening together, and an eight-year-old had ruined it.

Anger snuck into him as he caught up to Cole just before he entered the playground area. "Cole," he said. "Please wait."

The boy looked over his shoulder and kept right on going. "Leave me alone."

Blake wanted to reach out and grab him, make him stop, but he didn't think it wise. He was surprised he could think at all, given how upset he'd become. He let Cole go until he came to a bench near the tennis courts, where he sat.

Blake approached slowly. "I know I'm not your father. I don't want to be."

"Yes, you do. I've seen you with my mom."

Embarrassment heated his face further. "What have you seen?" Blake crouched in the wood chips in front of Cole, trying to make himself smaller. It wasn't easy with his height, but Cole didn't seem like he was about to run again.

"You kiss her after she puts us to bed."

Blake nodded, his eyes staying evenly on Cole's. "I like her. That's what grown-ups do when they like each other."

"She already has us. She doesn't need you."

"Of course she doesn't." Blake wasn't sure why he was agreeing with a child. "She loves you. She's not going to love you less by loving me." Blake shook his head. "I mean, not that she loves me. We're just...dating."

"If she wants us to do things as a family, I don't see why you get to come."

"Cole—"

"Leave us alone." The boy got up and Blake did grab him this time. "I already have a dad, and he's a lot better than you."

"Cole, I'm not trying to replace your dad, or you, or anyone."

"Let me go." He tried to wrench his arm free, but Blake was significantly stronger and the boy's struggle barely registered against the grip.

"Not until you understand—"

Cole screamed. A horrible, high-pitched scream that would surely draw the attention of everyone in the town.

Blake released him and watched him sprint away, his pulse bobbing somewhere behind his ears. A couple of mothers looked his way, but he ignored them and sat on the bench. In the distance, the bass notes from the concert could be heard.

Blake's thoughts had scattered and he couldn't seem to find them. *Shouldn't have disciplined her child*, he thought.

Cole's right.

You're not his dad.

Blake heaved a sigh as he stood. No matter what, no matter if he and Erin got married, no matter how many times he took Cole fishing, Blake would never be Cole's father. He walked away from the concert with those thoughts tumbling through his mind.

He left the park and started down the block away from Main Street, where the bakery stood. In order to walk around the entire park and get back to the bakery, where he'd parked his truck, he'd have to cover a couple of miles at least.

As he made the journey, he ignored the buzzing of his phone until it drove him mad. Then he silenced it. He didn't know what to tell Erin, and seeing as how Cole had run toward the concert instead of away from it, he figured the boy had made it back to her just fine.

He still didn't have the right words to say when he reached his truck, so he drove up the canyon, turned off his phone, and dropped to his knees beside his bed.

For a problem this big, he definitely needed divine help.

The following morning, Blake called Erin a few hours before he usually met her for church.

"Blake," she said, her voice on the outer edge of angry. "What is going on? I called you a bunch of times last night, and nothing? I get nothing from you?"

"I'm sorry," he said, his voice ringing with apology in the morning air behind his cabin. "I needed some time to think."

"And have you?"

"Yeah." He exhaled, his next words well-practiced and the ones he knew he needed to say. He just couldn't get himself to say them.

"And?" she prompted.

"Erin, I—I don't think we should see each other anymore."

The silence coming through the line testified that she hadn't expected him to say that. The fissures that had started in his heart last night widened into full-blown cracks.

"Why not?" she whispered.

He didn't want to blame the break-up on her. She didn't deserve that, had done nothing wrong. He absolutely wouldn't put it on her eight-year-old son. Which left one person. "I'm not ready," he said. "See, there's this girl I fell in love with in high school, and I thought I was over her, I swear I did. But I'm not." The story of his insane crush on Jessica poured from him, and while they weren't true, he could shoulder the blame for ending this relationship.

He finally stopped talking. Problem was, Erin didn't say anything either. He glanced at the phone, and the call was still connected.

"Erin?"

"What's her name?"

"Who?"

"This girl you're still in love with from high school." Erin spoke in a freaky calm voice Blake had only ever heard her use on Cole when he was misbehaving.

"Jessica Charles."

"Blake—" A sound very much like a sob came through the line, and Blake hung his head. He did not want to upset Erin. He never wanted to add more to her burdens.

"Blake, tell me this has nothing to do with Cole."

"Of course it doesn't." He was relieved she wasn't here to see his expression, because he was sure she'd be able to discover his lie.

"Because he said he'd apologize to you at church today."

"That's not necessary."

"You won't come to church today, will you?"

"I think I'll be there," Blake said.

"Great, we'll see you there."

"Erin, I—" He pressed his eyes closed and swallowed. "I don't want to sit by you."

The sniffling entering his ear was definitely crying this time. "Blake, please don't—"

"I have to go." He hung up and gripped his phone so tight it made his knuckles ache. He tossed it a few feet away in the grass, catching Rosco's attention. He went over to the device and sniffed it. Blake breathed rapidly, trying to figure out how he could live with this band of tension around his chest for the rest of his life.

Chapter 12

"Let's go visit Grandma and Grandpa," Erin announced as soon as she'd deemed herself presentable enough to leave the bedroom where Blake had just broken up with her. After hanging up, she'd cried into her pillow for a good ten minutes. Then she'd showered, hoping the hot water would erase the evidence of her puffy eyes.

With more makeup on than she normally wore, she bustled into the kitchen, which still wasn't put back together. Doug had ordered a new refrigerator and apparently it had gone out of stock, and Blake hadn't had time to get the walls patched and textured and painted yet.

"Grandma?" McKenzie asked, and Erin turned toward her. "That's right. Come on, guys. We haven't seen them since we moved out, and I don't feel like going to church today."

"No church?" Cole's eyes lit up. He whooped and ran toward the bedroom he shared with Davy.

Several minutes later, Erin drove away from Brush

Creek, finally able to draw a decent breath. She couldn't stand the thought of seeing Blake at church and not sitting by him. What was she supposed to do? Sit on the back row with her kids all alone?

She shook her head and gripped the steering wheel, oscillating between the need to cry and the need to punch something. With her emotions bombarding her thoughts, the drive to Vernal passed in a snap.

She pulled up to her parents' house, hoping her mother had stuck something in the Crock Pot, as she usually did in the summer months. Sure enough, the smell of marinara sauce met her nose when she pushed through the front door.

"Mom? Dad?"

The sliding glass door opened, and her father appeared. A sob worked its way up her throat, just as it had when she'd shown up in this very house the day she'd left Jeremy.

"Erin?" He turned back to the backyard. "It's Erin." Her mother followed her father, and several minutes passed with hugs and laughter and smiles. Erin did her best to join in, but all the joviality exhausted her.

"You're just in time for the irrigating," her dad said, and Davy cheered, dancing around like watering the lawn was the greatest thing on the planet. Erin had to admit it was pretty cool. Her dad would open the irrigation floodgate, and the entire backyard would fill with about six inches of water. He did it once a week, and the lawn stayed green and lush.

And her kids loved to wade in the flood, lay down in it, and as Davy liked to do, make "water angels."

He pranced up to her, his demeanor darkening. "We didn't bring our swimsuits."

She smoothed his hair. "Just take your shirt off, baby. We can throw your shorts in the dryer. I'm sure Grandpa has a shirt you can wear while they dry."

"I have their pajamas in the drawer in the bathroom," her mom said.

Erin forced a smile in her mom's direction. "Even better."

"So we can go?" Cole waited with his hand on the handle of the sliding glass door.

"Go," Erin said. Her father followed the kids into the yard, leaving Erin alone with her mother.

"What brings you here?" her mom asked, busying herself in the kitchen. She opened a bag of rolls and started slicing them. "How's the bakery?"

Erin sat at the counter and watched her mom for a few moments. "Aunt Shirley has me making all the pies now. She doesn't come in until five, and she only does the tarts."

"She called yesterday." Her mom flashed her a quick smile. "Told me you're doing great there." She paused in her work and trained her eyes on Erin's. "Do you like it?"

"You know what? I do like it." She wasn't sure if it mattered if she liked it. The job at the bakery paid the bills, and she had her own place to raise her kids. Her gaze wandered to the glass door and the three little people beyond it. "I came today because I didn't want to go to church."

"No?"

Erin shook her head, her tears getting dislodged. "The man I've been seeing broke up with me, and I—" She sniffed and wiped her eyes, shaking her head some more. She studied the countertop, wishing she hadn't gotten so attached to Blake.

Her mom laid the knife on the counter, her lunch preparations stalled. "You were seeing someone?"

"Dating, yes." Erin covered her face with her hands and took a deep, deep breath. "I don't remember breaking up feeling this bad." She lowered her hands and looked at her mom with raw emotion streaming from her. Her chin shook as she said, "Even ending things with Jeremy didn't feel like this."

Her mom gazed at her with eyes full of compassion. "Things with Jeremy had been over for a long time by the time you officially ended it."

"No, I know." Erin got up and tore a paper towel off the roll to wipe her eyes and nose.

"You must've really liked this new guy." Her mom leaned against the counter, watching Erin.

"I did, I guess," Erin said. "I mean, yeah, I did. I—" She drew in a shuddering breath. "We've been dating for a few months is all. He works at the ranch outside of town, and he's a general contractor too. Doug hired him to work on the bakery, and we've been—we've been spending time together and...and...." She trailed off as she realized she wanted to spend all her free time with Blake. She wanted him at her side at church, at home, all the time.

She gasped and covered her mouth with her hand. "And I fell in love with him." She spun toward the front door, like Blake would be standing there, a dozen roses in his hand.

"You fell in love with him?"

Erin locked eyes with her mom, completely dumbstruck herself. "I think I did."

Her mom's eyes shone and she smiled with true happiness. "That's wonderful, dear. Your father and I have been hoping you'd find someone again."

The feeling of elation that had been rising through her chest stalled, stopped, exploded. "But he just broke up with me."

"All right." Her mom picked up the knife and resumed cutting the rolls. "Tell me what happened, and let's figure this out."

So Erin took her seat at the bar again and started talking, ending with, "He said he wasn't over some girl he'd been in love with since high school."

Before her mom could offer what Erin was sure would solve all her problems, Cole led the kids and her dad back into the house. Things got loud for several minutes while towels were handed out, and hair dried, and clothes changed. Erin tossed all the wet clothes in the dryer and glanced to the plaque hanging on the wall above it.

Our greatest weakness lies in giving up.

Erin read it again, and again. She thought about Blake. Had he given up on them? Because of her? Because of Cole? Because of this Jessica woman?

Would Erin give up on them?

"I don't want to," she whispered to herself. Her love might be new, fledgling, trying to grow real wings, but it existed inside her heart. She couldn't give up on Blake because he had a decade-old crush.

"What should I do?" she asked as she steadied herself against the dryer.

Find out who Jessica Charles is.

With a plan and renewed determination, Erin returned to the kitchen, where she whispered to her mom about her idea to look up this other woman and then talk to Blake about how she felt.

"Doable?" she asked as her mom put the finishing touches on the pasta.

"Definitely doable." Her mom gave her a quick squeeze. "Call me when you know anything. After you talk to him. Anytime."

―――

Finding Jessica Charles was harder than Erin thought it would be. Probably because her computer was as old as Davy, and the Internet at the bakery needed to be updated. Her kids had gone to bed an hour ago, and she felt like a modern female MacGyver as she brought up a couple of search windows.

She knew Blake had grown up in Colorado, and she found sixteen Jessica's in his graduating class. None of them had the last name of Charles.

Perplexed, she started at the top of the list with Jessica Anderson and turned to Facebook. A lot of women—Erin herself included—used their maiden names when they got married. But nothing made sense, because why would Blake still be hung up on a girl from ten years ago who'd gotten married?

Confused but undaunted, Erin searched until she found a Jessica Jeffries Charles. She couldn't see a whole lot of information, but she could see that she'd graduated from the same high school as Blake.

"Can't be coincidence," she muttered to herself. She wanted to see everything about this Jessica Charles, get all the facts, make the best case she could for why Blake needed to leave this other woman in the past.

She clicked the "Add Friend" button even though she and Jessica didn't have a single friend in common. Her mind ran through that information. Jessica wasn't even friends with Blake.

"Maybe he's not on Facebook." She clicked and searched and scanned, and sure enough, she found a Blake Gibbons with a profile picture of him riding a bull. Upon further examination, she realized that it couldn't be Blake, but had to be his twin brother.

She wasn't sure how she felt about Blake's misrepresentation of himself, but then she realized that the last time he'd posted had been over a year ago. He obviously didn't use the social media platform much and she didn't want to judge him on a photograph. Maybe he was just proud of his brother. She'd put pictures of her kids up as her profile picture before.

Satisfied she had a good start to the information she needed, she shut down the computer and went to bed. She paused by the sleeping form of McKenzie, love rushing through her for the little girl. She'd thought Kenz would be her miracle baby, the one that would heal all the rifts in her marriage with Jeremy.

How foolish she'd been. For a few months after the divorce, Erin had trouble adoring her little girl. She still loved her, but looking into McKenzie's eyes—the same shade of navy blue as Jeremy's—had sometimes made her breath cut through her chest.

She felt none of that now, thankfully.

Erin sent a prayer of gratitude up to God for His help over the past year. She added, And help me know what to do with Blake. What to tell him. What to say to bring him back to me.

As she stood there in the brown-black darkness, she realized she'd never prayed for help to fix her broken relationship with Jeremy. Maybe she hadn't had enough faith. Maybe she hadn't really wanted to repair the marriage. No matter what *maybe* was true, Erin knew she didn't want to give up this time.

Chapter 13

Blake didn't see Erin and her kids at church that day. Or the next week. He missed church for the following two weekends due to harvesting. And he was behind due to his main harvester throwing its chain. He'd spent hours in the machinery shed trying to figure out how to get it up and running again.

He hadn't been able to, and Walker didn't want him taking a day to get to Salt Lake to *maybe* find the part they needed. His argument of it needing to be special-ordered had merit, and Blake woke before the sun so he could get the numbers he needed to call in an order.

He stomped across the street and around the homestead, the weather growing cooler and cooler each morning. He pulled his jacket tighter as he entered the machinery shed, surprised to find Walker there with his son Michael.

"Good morning," Walker said.

Blake grunted. He'd found very little to be good about the past twenty-seven mornings since he'd called Erin and ended things between them. He hated the way his phone sat silent most of the time now. Hated the way he hadn't finished the job at the bakery the way he'd said he would. He'd told Doug that he'd be back to finish everything up once the harvest was over, but guilt still needled him whenever he thought about Erin—which was all the time.

He knew, though, that those thoughts would eventually be replaced with new ones. After all, he'd felt like this after Jessica had dated everyone but him, gone to college, had gotten engaged and then married. The thoughts always faded; the pain always hurt for a while and then got better; the memories always played in full color in his dreams and then dulled. He just needed more time.

Time.

Erin had wanted time.

Blake shook his head, realizing that Walker was watching him. "I'm sorry. Did you say something?"

"Wondered how Erin's kids were liking school now that it's started."

"I don't know." Blake looked right at Walker, sure the foreman already knew they'd broken up. Ted hadn't exactly been quiet about Blake not sitting on the back row during church while they loaded hay into the loft last week. And Tess had brought Blake a chocolate cake on Saturday night for no reason at all.

"What are you guys doing here so early?" Blake asked in an attempt to change the subject.

"I'm takin' the boys down to school this morning, so I thought I'd get some things done before that."

Blake nodded and walked over to the combine harvester that had made this fall one of the worst. He climbed into the driver's seat and pulled out the owner's manual. A few inches thick, the manual seemed daunting to Blake when it normally wouldn't.

Everything had seemed harder since Erin's departure from his life.

It was your choice, he told himself in the sternest thought possible. You *chose to end things with her.*

He leafed through the book, looking for the section on augers so he could find the part numbers he needed. Twenty minutes later, with the snapshot of it on his phone, he climbed down from the harvester to find the machinery shed empty. Relief flooded him. He didn't want a lecture from Walker. Walker, who had more strength than anyone else on the ranch. Who had raised a son by himself for several years before remarrying. Who always gave advice Blake heeded.

He exited the shed only to find Walker leaning against it. "There you are."

"Jeez." Blake jumped away in surprise, his heart kicking into a new gear from the adrenaline. "You scared me." He kept walking toward his cabin, but he knew he couldn't out-stride Walker.

"I wanted to talk to you about Erin."

"Not interested."

"In her? Or in talking to me about her?"

Blake stopped on the cusp of the dirt road that led back to the lane and separated the homestead on the south from the fields on the north. "Both." He daggered Walker with a look that said *Drop it*, and started walking again.

"Okay, don't talk back then." Walker matched him step for step. "Just listen."

"I don't want to be talked at either."

"Well, someone has to tell you what you're missin'."

"What's that?"

"You like Erin Shields, right?"

"I think it would be impossible not to like Erin Shields."

"Yeah, but I like her in a different way than you do."

"If you say so." Blake's cabin came into view, with Rosco waiting for him on the front porch.

"Can't you see how miserable you are?" Walker darted in front of him, blocking Blake's escape. "I can, and it's makin' everyone around here miserable."

"Name one person."

"Emmett. Ted. Me. Justin. Grant. Even Landon said you snapped at him a few days ago."

"I did not." At least Blake couldn't think of when he'd have done that. Landon was his boss; Landon signed his paycheck. Blake had never had a problem with the man. Liked working for him. Found him to be a fair boss.

"He said you told him you needed more help for the harvest." Ted's right eyebrow cocked. "In no uncertain terms."

"We do need more cowhands for the harvest. There are men who'll come just for two weeks—or less, because with more help, the harvest wouldn't take so long."

"Yeah, but you can't boss around the boss."

"I didn't. I was making a suggestion."

"Didn't sound like it."

Blake spun toward the new voice, finding Landon standing there, his jeans, cowboy boots, and brown leather jacket standard ranch wear in the autumn. Between him and Walker, the only difference was the color of their cowboy hats. Blake sighed. "I'm sorry, Landon. I've been...."

"Moody," Landon supplied at the same time Walker said, "Grouchy."

"Am I not getting my work done?" Blake challenged.

"No, you're doin' just fine," Landon said, gazing past him toward the fields. "Only a couple more days, from what Walker said."

"Mowing the last fields today," Blake confirmed. "It's just slow."

"Not everything has to be done quickly," Landon said. "Maybe you just need to give yourself more time to figure things out with Erin."

"It's not Erin," Blake said, wondering how they'd gone from mowing hay to women in less than a breath.

"No?" Walker asked, exchanging a glance with Landon that Blake didn't like.

He shook his head, the fight in his body leaving. He'd told Erin it was him, that he wasn't over Jessica. But that wasn't true. It was him, but it had nothing to do with Erin or Jessica.

"It's her kids," he said, everything in him admitting defeat. He'd wanted to tell someone, but he didn't want to come off as a selfish jerk.

"Her kids?" Walker asked, his eyes harboring a dark edge. "What about them?"

"I don't think I'm ready to take on a family of five," he said. "Three of which are under the age of eight."

"Better than three under the age of four," Landon grumbled.

Walker chuckled and Blake managed a smile. "Her oldest son doesn't like me much."

"You haven't spent much time with him," Walker said. "You've got to give it more than a month."

"And not even a month," Landon said. "A month of weekends."

Blake's lungs stormed, barely able to hold oxygen. He breathed, trying to make them function properly. They finally complied, right before he felt like passing out. "He said I'll never be his father."

"And you won't," Walker agreed. "It's hard to build a new family from parts of an old one, but it can be done. Tess and I manage okay."

"It's different for you," Blake said. "You had a kid, and so did Tess, and they're both boys, and they get along great, and—"

"They don't always get along great," Walker said. "Trust me."

"Nothing about having a family is easy," Landon agreed.

"You're not making a very strong case here, guys," Blake said. "And I've got a phone call to make."

He stepped past Walker, almost making it to the front door before his friend called out, "Give yourself more time, Blake!"

He raised his hand to indicate he'd heard, but he entered the cabin without looking back. As he made the phone call and ordered the part, as he grabbed his leather gloves and headed back across the street to get the operational harvester going, he couldn't help thinking *More time for what?*

His phone showed one missed call when Blake made it in from the fields. Everything had gotten mowed, just as he'd said it would. Now the hay would dry for a couple of days, and he'd get out there and bale it. Then he'd go over the fields one more time to pick up the bales, and with a few hours work, the hayloft would be full. The harvest would be over. Finally.

He dialed Doug back, his stomach growling for something more than a protein bar to eat. Problem was, he didn't have much more available at home.

"Hey, Blake."

"You called?"

"That refrigerator finally came in." He let the sentence hang there, the unspoken part of it loud and clear.

"Great," Blake said, his gut rebelling against the idea of stepping foot inside the bakery. "I'll be down tomorrow to finish everything up." He entered the cabin and gave Rosco a scrub behind his ears. "How's everything else holding up at the bakery?"

"Just great," Doug said.

"Great." Blake sighed with relief. "I'll see you tomorrow then."

He wished tomorrow wouldn't come, but it did. It always did. He cleared it with Walker to go down to the bakery that morning, a wild idea that had struck Blake as he lay in bed the previous night. Maybe if he went in the morning, he wouldn't see Erin.

He pulled into the parking lot, which seemed unusually busy for a Tuesday, and entered through the side door that allowed access to her apartment and the kitchen. His heart seized, thinking of the last time he'd used this door. He glanced left, up the stairs, his pulse beating against the back of his tongue.

"How long on the key lime tarts?" Erin's voice floated to him from the kitchen, and Blake froze. He'd almost forgotten the sound of her voice, the smell of her skin, but it all rushed back at him now.

Move, he told himself as Shirley said something. He went upstairs, making his bootsteps as quiet as possible. Her apartment was surprisingly clean, and McKenzie sat on the couch, watching a cartoon. She glanced up at Blake and a smile burst onto her face.

"Blake," she said in her simple voice.

"Hello, sweet girl." He gave her a smile and tousled her hair as he moved past her and into the kitchen. His heart squeezed with the affection he felt for McKenzie. His life narrowed to just this apartment and the good times he'd had here. He set down his tool kit and headed back to the door.

"I've gotta grab my painting stuff," he said to McKenzie. "Okay?"

"'Kay," she said, her focus back on the TV.

Blake made another trip down the stairs and back up without hearing or seeing Erin. He allowed himself to breathe normally once he was in the apartment with McKenzie again, the door closed.

He assessed the work he'd done and what was left to finish. He'd hung the new sheetrock, but it hadn't been sealed and patched to the old walls. He also needed to texture and then paint before installing the new refrigerator, which almost blocked the hallway leading to the bedrooms and the bathroom.

He'd barely finished patching the wall into a seamless surface when the door opened behind him.

"Hey, Kenz, you doing okay?"

Blake turned toward the magical sound of Erin's voice, and their eyes met. Hers widened and she lifted one hand to press it over her heart. "Blake."

"Hello, Erin," he forced out of his mouth. Every nerve ending in his body fired hot and fast. "Just finishing this up for you—for *Doug*—today. You'll have your kitchen back in order by lunchtime."

Her gaze flew to the computer desk, which held stacks of mail and a couple of notebooks, maybe some homework now that the kids were back in school. "I—I just came to check on Kenz."

"I'll keep an eye on her," Blake said, turning back to the project at hand. He simply stared at the wall, wondering how he could eliminate this awkwardness between him and Erin. He lived here; so did she. Would it be like this every time he saw her? At church, the bakery, the park, everywhere?

"Thanks," Erin said.

Blake turned, hopeful that Erin hadn't left yet. She hadn't even moved. She blinked; so did he.

"Listen, Erin." He swallowed. "I'm—"

"If you're going to apologize again, please don't." Even from across the apartment, Blake saw the anger in her eyes.

"Okay," he said stupidly. He didn't know what to say now, but he did want to make her life easier not harder. Maybe he did need more time with her, with Cole, before he could decide if this relationship was going to work or not.

"Are you headed back up to the ranch after you finish here?" she asked, her voice back to normal.

"Yeah. I have to settle up with Doug, and then yeah. I have work to do on the ranch."

"Do you have time for dinner this week?"

Shock traveled through Blake. "I—I suppose."

"Which night?" she pressed.

His mind had blanked the moment he'd seen her. He still held the scraper he'd been using, and it hung at his side uselessly. "I don't know."

"Tonight?"

He couldn't think of a reason why not. He couldn't think of anything. "I guess."

A smile touched her lips, and Blake's attention fell there. All the emotions he'd felt for Erin broke through the layer of plastic wrap he'd been using to keep them at bay.

"Great," she said. "I'll bring some pizza. We can talk." She nodded once as if to say *that was that* and left the apartment.

Chapter 14

When Erin arrived at Blake's cabin, she thought her heart would fly right out of her chest. Another man opened the front door and led Rosco outside on a leash. She didn't recognize the other cowboy, but he went next door to the cabin on the end, taking the dog with him.

Erin grabbed the pot of spaghetti she'd made, along with a grocery sack containing a bagged salad and some garlic breadsticks from the bakery. She marched right up to the cabin door and knocked.

Blake opened it, his bright blue eyes assessing her from head to toe. "Hey. That doesn't look like pizza." The half smirk on his face touched her heart. How she'd missed that look that he seemed to reserve only for her.

"I had to feed the kids, so I made spaghetti."

He glanced behind her. "You didn't bring them?"

"Aunt Shirley is watching them." She nodded toward the interior of the house. "Can I come in?"

He stepped back and reached for the grocery sack. "You didn't have to feed me."

"I didn't think you'd come down the canyon for a second time in one day." She entered his cabin and took a deep breath. She'd always loved the smell of him—musky and woody and warm, with a hint of mint.

He closed the door behind her, his tall frame making her feel small and claustrophobic in the cabin. She moved away from him and set the spaghetti on the kitchen counter. "Let's eat first."

"What are we going to do second?" He set the rest of the groceries on the counter.

She pulled the salad and breadsticks out of the bag before pinning him with a look. "We're going to talk."

He swallowed visibly, and while she felt the same fear tugging through her, she didn't think she could survive without him for much longer. She had the facts she needed. She just needed to lay them out and see what he said.

He got down two plates and she filled them with food. He asked her about the kids, and school, and the bakery. She filled the silence with pleasantries and updates, dancing around the harder topics until he was well-fed.

Finally, he sat back from his plate. "You do make a great batch of spaghetti and meatballs." His warm smile gave her hope. He may have broken up with her, but the flame between them burned as hot as ever.

She got up from the table and retrieved her purse from where she'd dropped it next to the front door. She withdrew the folder she needed and sat on the couch, giving him a pointed look.

He joined her but sat on the opposite end from her

when she wanted him right next to her. "I looked up Jessica Charles," she said.

He sucked in a breath with a sharp hiss. "You did what?"

"She's married, Blake. She lives in California, and she's due with her first baby—a son—in only nine weeks."

A range of emotions crossed his face, from anger to fear to defiance to acceptance, all in a single heartbeat.

Erin lifted her chin and looked straight into those blue eyes she loved. "She says you two haven't spoken in years. I think you lied to me." She cocked her head to the side and asked, "Have you lied to me, Blake?"

To his credit, he didn't even try to deny it. He nodded and said, "Yeah."

Her pulse pinched. "Why?"

"I didn't lie when I said I wasn't ready. Just the reason why."

"I know you love me," she said next. She didn't know but the way he sighed and softened testified that he did.

"I'm sorry, Erin. I tried not to fall so fast. You said you needed time, and then things went bad between me and Cole...." He shrugged and studied his hands.

"Things didn't go bad at all," she said, opening the folder. "I asked him to write you a note." She passed over the single sheet of paper, which Blake took with an edge of curiosity on his face.

He didn't look at it. "He told me I'd never be his father. He's right."

"I don't need you to be his father," Erin said, suddenly regretting her idea to eat before talking as her stomach revolted against the spaghetti she'd consumed. "I need you to be my husband."

Blake blinked once, twice. "I'm sorry. What?"

Erin slid down the couch until her knee almost touched Blake's. "This folder has my chats with Jessica, confirming you went out with her once, almost ten years ago. I believe you liked her, but I don't believe for a single second she's the reason we can't be together."

"She's not," Blake whispered. "I'm over her. I got over her the moment I met you."

Erin's heart bumped irregularly in her chest. "I have some pictures Davy and McKenzie drew for you. Davy asks about you everyday, and I'm tired of making up excuses for why you stopped coming around."

"I'll talk to him," Blake said. "I'm sorry he feels bad." He ducked his head, and Erin reached up and removed his cowboy hat, everything almost laid out. Good thing, too, because she was dying to kiss him.

"I talked to Cole, and he'll...take a little longer to come around, but it isn't because he doesn't like you. It's because there's a lot going on in his life right now." She nodded to the letter. "You should read it."

Blake set it on the coffee table in front of him. "Later."

"I love you," Erin said. "So you can't use me as an excuse. Or Jessica, or McKenzie, or Davy, or Cole. So that only leaves one person, Blake." She touched his chest, fiddled with a button on his shirt. "You."

Blake ducked his head again, and Erin trailed her fingers across his scalp. He shivered at her touch, causing her to smile. "I don't want to give up on us," she whispered. "So just tell me what the problem is, and we'll figure it out."

He raised his eyes to her and they were filled with agony. "Me, Erin," he said. "*I'm* the problem."

Confusion poured through her. She'd debunked the myth about Jessica. Spoken to her children. Gotten him to confess that he loved her. "How so?"

"I don't know if I'm ready to have a family," he said. "Do you even think the five of us will fit in this cabin?" He gestured to the space around them. The living room held a couch and a loveseat just fine. The kitchen had a bar and a table—lots of places to eat. He had two bedrooms and a loft. A big, wide playground of land, streams, and hills for the kids. Even a dog.

"Of course we will," Erin said, cradling his face in her palm. "I know I come with a lot."

"You don't just come with a lot," he said. "Three kids, Erin. I have to know how to take care of them right now. No time to learn. No time to adjust. I'm terrified I'll make a lot of mistakes."

She smiled tenderly at him and put her other hand on the other side of his face. "Do you think I know what I'm doing? There's no manual for this. And besides, you don't have to do it alone."

"You really think we can figure this out?"

Hope burst through her. "I know we can."

"I love you," he whispered just before touching his lips to hers.

Giddiness made her pulse race and her lips curve upward. "I love you too." This time when he kissed her, it held all the old passion she'd felt in his touch before. Something new too, because she knew he loved her and she loved him.

Ten Months Later

"That mattress goes in the loft," Blake said to Landon, who'd shown up first to help move Erin and her children into the cabin.

"This must be yours," the tough cowboy said to McKenzie as he shouldered the toddler-sized mattress.

She grinned at him like he was a superhero. "Mama says I get my own bed now." She traipsed off with Landon, where they entered the house together.

Blake looked in the fifteen-foot truck, overwhelmed as only a handful of items had been removed from it. He wasn't sure how all of this stuff was going to fit into his thousand-square-foot cabin, but he kept his thoughts to himself as he went up the ramp and grabbed onto a lamp.

"Blake!" Davy danced out of the cabin, his face a picture of pure delight. "The bedroom is amazing. Even Cole said so."

Blake grinned. "I'm glad you boys like it." He'd spent the last three weeks remodeling it with new paint, new curtains, and a floor that would withstand two boys living in it. He'd downgraded his office and moved it into the bedroom he'd share with Erin once they were married.

Only one more day, he thought as she came out of the house wearing a smile the size of the Mississippi River. He hurried down the ramp and took her into his arms. "I missed you," he murmured into her ear.

She tilted her head back, which only gave him better access to her neck, and laughed. "We've been gone for a week."

Blake kissed her, cutting the contact short when he heard footsteps approaching from inside the house. He stepped back from Erin and met Cole's eye. "Did you have fun in California?"

Cole grinned and bent down to pat Rosco. "It was awesome. Have you been to the ocean?"

"Couple of times," Blake said.

"Mom says we can go again next year."

"She did, huh?" He glanced at Erin. "Did she tell you where we're goin' after we get married tomorrow?"

"No." Cole pouted and picked up a ball to throw for the dog. "She still won't say anything."

"Good." Blake grinned. "Now let's get this truck unloaded." Cole and Davy were decent workers, and all the cowboys showed up in the next several minutes, making short work of the furniture and boxes in the truck.

The bunk bed got assembled, and Megan showed up with lunch, and Tess led the other ranch wives in helping Erin unpack more towels and sheets and clothes than Blake knew were required.

"So, where are you taking everyone tomorrow?" Landon asked as they stood on the front porch and watched the four boys that now lived at the ranch run down the dirt road, three dogs with them.

"Yellowstone," Blake said. "Cole and Davy love to camp. They're sleeping in a tent in Shirley's yard tonight."

"Is that where Erin's staying too?"

"Yeah." Blake watched her tuck her hair behind her ear, a rush of affection for her flooding him.

"So you'll be a family tomorrow."

The thought didn't frighten him as it had for months. At some point, while the snow obscured the landscape, he'd found peace with being a father of three and a husband all on the same day. "Yeah."

Erin came to the door and started to close it. "I'm getting out my wedding dress," she explained. "No peeking. It's bad luck to see the bride in her dress before the wedding."

Blake raised his hands in acquiescence, though he wanted nothing more than to see her in that dress because it would mean they were about to be married, and he'd been waiting for many long months for that.

THE NEXT DAY, Blake fidgeted like someone had lit the outside layer of his skin on fire. He scratched, he pulled on his tie, he paced until Walker came to get him. Once inside the chapel, the anxiety intensified. Erin wasn't there, and neither were her children or her parents. Shirley and Johnny sat in the second row, along with Doug and his family.

Blake's parents and siblings sat on the opposite side of the aisle, and Blake held his mom tight when she hugged him. "I'm so happy for you," she said. He knew his brother and sister had sacrificed to be there, as rodeo season was in high gear. He embraced them too and then straightened his cowboy hat and swallowed as he looked toward the back of the chapel.

Erin's parents appeared and moved swiftly down the aisle. He'd met them several times over the course of the months, and he liked them.

All at once, McKenzie appeared, holding a silver wire basket. She stepped forward and tossed white petals as the wedding march started up on the organ.

Erin filled the doorway, making Blake's breath seize in his chest. He'd never seen anything or anyone quite so beautiful in all his days. Her dress clung to her body, fanning out in layer upon layer from the waist down. She wore her hair in a big knot on the back of her head, and she absolutely radiated happiness as she stepped forward with Davy escorting her on the right and Cole on the left.

She reached the front of the chapel and kissed both of her sons on their foreheads before linking her arm in Blake's. He could hardly believe this day had arrived, could hardly fathom how he'd gotten this gorgeous, strong, faithful woman to agree to be his.

He glanced at the stained glass window behind the pastor as the ceremony started. He'd found a lot of things in this chapel. His own relationship with God. A community of people to belong to. Erin and her kids.

They were pronounced man and wife, and Blake kissed Erin like he'd never kissed her before. Because this was the first kiss of the rest of their lives, and he wanted it to be special. This kiss was the start of their family, and Blake wanted to remember it forever.

The crowd applauded, and Blake gestured for McKenzie, Davy, and Cole to come forward so they could all walk together out of the chapel as a family.

Joy filled him with every step, and as he helped Erin and the children into his truck, he said, "All right guys. Off on our first family adventure."

"Where are we going?" Cole asked, and Blake grinned at him.

"You'll see."

The boy groaned, and Blake fully expected him to whine and argue on this trip. For Davy to annoy him, and for McKenzie to need to stop to go to the bathroom a dozen times before they reached Yellowstone.

But he didn't care. They were his family now, and he loved them.

Read on for a sneak peek of **THE COWBOY AND THE CHAMPION**, the next book in the Brush Creek Cowboys series!

Sneak Peek! The Cowboy and the Champion Chapter One

"Landon?" Emmett Graves entered the homestead at Brush Creek Horse Ranch just after five o'clock on a Friday afternoon. He'd been told by the foreman that the owner wanted to see him before the weekend. So here he was.

Landon, apparently, was not at the homestead, as Megan poked her head up from the kitchen cabinets where she crouched. "Hey, Emmett." She gave him a smile and disappeared again.

He moved through the living room, past a set of stairs that went down, and into the kitchen, where he found Megan organizing plastic storage containers and nesting them inside each other.

"Where's Landon?"

"He hasn't come in from the ranch yet." She glanced up at him. "What do you need?"

"He wanted me to stop by." A sense of urgency trickled through Emmett. He wanted to shower, grab something to eat, and get down to town. The country line dances had been going for a couple of weeks now, and he'd enjoyed himself at them.

"I'll text him." She stood and sent a message to her husband. "You goin' dancin' tonight?"

He laughed. "Don't talk like a cowboy," he said. "You can't even pull it off."

"Yes, I can." She slugged him in the shoulder. "So are you going?"

"Yep."

"You meet anyone down there?"

"Oh, don't start on me." Emmett groaned. "Between you and Tess it's a miracle I don't have a date every other night."

"Do you want a date every other night?" Megan's dark eyes glittered. "Because I know a lot of women that would be interested."

"*I'm* not interested," Emmett said. Megan tilted her head and looked at him with curiosity, but Landon entered the house through the French doors, saving Emmett from trying to explain.

Trying to explain was all he could do. No one really understood his aversion to women—not even Emmett himself. All he knew was that women couldn't be trusted. They didn't stick around when things got hard. His momma had left when he was twelve, and he hadn't heard from her since.

His father had been married and divorced three times, and both of Emmett's older brothers had endured divorces as well.

No thank you, Emmett thought as Landon washed his hands.

The fact that the owner hadn't said anything upon his arrival set Emmett's alert on high. "Ted said you wanted to see me before the weekend," he said.

"Right," Landon said, exchanging a glance with Megan. He sighed, further worrying Emmett.

"I've hired another trainer."

"That's great," Emmett said, trying to find the hidden meaning in the words. Or hear words Landon hadn't said at all.

"They'll be doing barrel racing as well. I need you to train them."

An icy wind swept through Emmett. "*They'll* be doing barrel racing? What will I be doing then?"

"Barrel racing."

Emmett's eyebrows pinched together. "So you'll have two barrel racing trainers?"

"For a while."

Emmett straightened his square shoulders. He wasn't as tall as Landon or some of the other cowboys on the ranch, but he could hold his own. "Am I being fired?"

"Of course not." Landon looked at Megan again, who came to stand at his side. A flash of resentment for their relationship stole through Emmett. At the same time, he envied them. "I'm just doin' a favor for a friend, and I need you to show them the ropes."

"When is this happening?"

"Monday." Landon held perfectly still, a tactic Emmett had seen him use before. It exuded confidence and the message that he wasn't going to budge on the topic at hand.

Emmett admitted defeat with an exaggerated sigh. "Fine. Is that all?"

"That's all. Just be here at the homestead at seven sharp on Monday morning."

Emmett saluted Landon, who rolled his eyes and said, "Get outta here."

WITH HIS TEETH brushed and his dark hair still a bit damp and curling on the ends, Emmett set his sights down the canyon. The temperature improved by a few degrees as he left the higher elevations behind. The dances were held at Oxbow Park, the largest outdoor venue Brush Creek had to offer.

The days were getting longer now that May was half over, and Emmett parked with several minutes of sunlight left. He made his way past the playground to a large pavilion which had been emptied of all the tables. Music pumped from the lit space, the kind of country twang that brought a quick smile to Emmett's face.

He didn't join the throng of people already on the cement dance floor right away. He stuck to the edges, checking out the dancers and finding his groove with the music. He chewed his arctic ice gum with vigor, his anticipation of expending some extra energy on the dance floor amping up.

"Hey, Emmett." A blonde-haired woman walked by, but Emmett barely glanced at her as he returned the greeting. He really wasn't interested in anything long-term with a female. But spending an evening dancing with one was perfectly fine.

He merged into the crowd during the song transition,

finding himself right next to a tall, curvy woman wearing jeans that went on forever. It was the jeans that should've tipped him off. Most of the other women there wore flirty little dresses, not jeans, black cowgirl boots, and a blouse the color of clouds.

He tapped the heel of his boot, then the toe, launching himself fully into the line dance. The redhead next to him had clearly missed the last several years of line dances, because she fumbled all over the place, even coming close to backing into him a time or two.

He chuckled and when the song ended, he said, "When's the last time you line danced?"

She trained her dazzling hazel eyes on him, and Emmett thought he might be really interested in dating her. "It's been a while," she admitted. Her gaze slid down his body and back to his cowboy hat, where her lip curled.

She had skin that had spent plenty of time in the sun. Freckles dotted her nose and cheeks, and her hair had to be naturally curly.

"I don't think we've met," he said. "I'm Emmett."

"We haven't." The woman turned and pushed her way through the crowd to a different section of the dance floor, leaving Emmett to stare after her.

He blinked and a laugh flew from his throat. Another song started, and Emmett kept his eye on the dancing disaster that was the redhead. Another man—sans cowboy hat—spoke to her, and she seemed perfectly warm with him.

Emmett's mood dampened, and he maneuvered toward the refreshment table. So what if that woman didn't like him? He wasn't looking for anyone either. He just thought if *he'd* nearly trampled someone, the least he could do was apologize. And if someone introduced themselves to him, his good Southern manners dictated that he introduce himself back.

The frustration over the nameless woman left him as he downed a cup of lemonade, the chill of it intensifying against the mint of his gum. He refilled his cup and faced the crowd again. There were lots of other women here to dance next to. He didn't need her.

He turned to put his nearly-full cup of lemonade in the trashcan but collided with another body. His grip on the plastic cup failed and the yellow liquid doused the woman he'd nearly knocked over.

Now her cloud-colored shirt looked like a dog had peed on it.

"I'm sorry," Emmett said as he picked up the empty cup and put it in his original target—the trashcan. He grabbed a fistful of napkins and started pawing at the woman's shirt.

She backed up and held up both of her hands. "Stop. Just...stop."

Emmett blinked, pure horror flowing through him at the distaste the woman wore on her face. Distaste for him. He wasn't sure what he'd done to make her dislike him so much—besides dumping ten ounces of ice cold lemonade down the front of her. But she'd seemed cold before then.

He forced a laugh and said, "So you can't dance, and I can't drink. Maybe we should both go home before we cause some real damage." He kept his genuine smile on his face. The smile he wore when he was trying to get something he wanted. The smile that always worked.

Almost always worked.

Because the redhead scoffed, spun away from him, and stomped out of the pavilion. Emmett followed her, pausing where the cement met the grass. "Wait!" he called. "I didn't get your number!"

She didn't even turn around, and Emmett faced the dance floor with a chuckle. That woman needed a chill pill, because it was only lemonade. It would come out in the wash, for crying out loud.

"You wanna dance?" The blonde parked herself in front of him, and Emmett figured *why not?*

"Sure." He gave that grin again, satisfied that it worked on some women. *Human women*, he thought as he scanned the darkness beyond the pavilion for the redhead. She was nowhere to be found, so he spun the blonde, and drank too much lemonade, and laughed good-naturedly until the dance ended near midnight.

Can Emmett and Molly get over their pasts in order to build a future together? Find out in **THE COWBOY AND THE CHAMPION - available now in ebook, paperback, and audiobook!**

Books in the Brush Creek Cowboy Romance Series:

Brush Creek Cowboy (Book 1): Former rodeo champion and cowboy Walker Thompson trains horses at Brush Creek Horse Ranch, where he lives a simple life in his cabin with his ten-year-old son. A widower of six years, he's worked with Tess Wagner, a widow who came to Brush Creek to escape the turmoil of her life to give her seven-year-old son a slower pace of life. But Tess's breast cancer is back...

Walker will have to decide if he'd rather spend even a short time with Tess than not have her in his life at all. Tess wants to feel God's love and power, but can she discover and accept God's will in order to find her happy ending?

The Cowboy's Challenge (Book 2): Cowboy and professional roper Justin Jackman has found solitude at Brush Creek Horse Ranch, preferring his time with the animals he trains over dating. With two failed engagements in his past, he's not really interested in getting his heart stomped on again. But when flirty and fun Renee  Martin picks him up at a church ice cream bar--on a bet, no less--he finds himself more than just a little interested. His Gen-X attitudes are attractive to her; her Millennial behaviors drive him nuts. Can Justin look past their differences and take a chance on another engagement?

A Cowboy Proposal (Book 3): Ted Caldwell has been a retired bronc rider for years, and he thought he was perfectly happy training horses to buck at Brush Creek Ranch. He was wrong. When he meets April Nox, who comes to the ranch to hide her pregnancy from all her friends back in Jackson Hole, Ted realizes he has a huge family-shaped hole in his life. April is embarrassed, heartbroken, and trying to find her extinguished faith. She's never ridden a horse and wants nothing to do with a cowboy ever again. Can Ted and April create a family of happiness and love from a tragedy?

A New Family for the Cowboy (Book 4): Blake Gibbons oversees all the agriculture at Brush Creek Horse Ranch, sometimes moonlighting as a general contractor. When he meets Erin Shields, new in town, at her aunt's bakery, he's instantly smitten. Erin moved to Brush Creek after a divorce that left her penniless, homeless, and a single mother of three children under age eight. She's nowhere near ready to start dating again, but the longer Blake hangs around the bakery, the more she starts to like him. Can Blake and Erin find a way to blend their lifestyles and become a family?

The Cowboy and the Champion (Book 5): Emmett Graves has always had a positive outlook on life. He adores training horses to become barrel racing champions during the day and cuddling with his cat at night. Fresh off her professional rodeo retirement, Molly Brady comes to Brush Creek Horse Ranch as Emmett's protege. He's not thrilled, and she's allergic to cats. Oh, and she'd like to stay cowboy-free, thank you very much. But Emmett's about as cowboy as they come.... Can Emmett and Molly work together without falling in love?

Schooled by the Cowboy (Book 6): Grant Ford spends his days training cattle—when he's not camped out at the elementary school hoping to catch a glimpse of his ex-girlfriend. When principal Shannon Sharpe confronts him and asks him to stay away from the school, the spark between them is instant and hot. Shan-

non's expecting a transfer very soon, but she also needs a summer outdoor coordinator—and Grant fits the bill. Just because he's handsome and everything Shannon's ever wanted in a cowboy husband means nothing. Will Grant and Shannon be able to survive the summer or will the Utah heat be too much for them to handle?

The Marine's Marriage: A Fuller Family Novel - Brush Creek Cowboys Romance (Book 1): Tate Benson can't believe he's come to Nowhere, Utah, to fix up a house that hasn't been inhabited in years. But he has. Because he's retired from the Marines and looking to start a life as a police officer in small-town Brush Creek. Wren Fuller has her hands full most days running her family's company. When Tate calls and demands a maid for that morning, she decides to have the calls forwarded to her cell and go help him out. She didn't know he was moving in next door, and she's completely unprepared for his handsomeness, his kind heart, and his wounded soul. **Can Tate and Wren weather a relationship when they're also next-door neighbors?**

The Firefighter's Fiancé: A Fuller Family Novel - Brush Creek Cowboys Romance (Book 2): Cora Wesley comes to Brush Creek, hoping to get some in-the-wild firefighting training as she prepares to put in her application to be a hotshot. When she meets Brennan Fuller, the spark between them is hot and instant.  As they get to know each other, her deadline is constantly looming over them, and Brennan starts to wonder if he can break ranks in the family business. He's okay mowing lawns and hanging out with his brothers, but he dreams of being able to go to college and become a landscape architect, but he's just not sure it can be done. **Will Cora and Brennan be able to endure their trials to find true love?**

The Trooper's Treasure: A Fuller Family Novel - Brush Creek Cowboys Romance (Book 3): Dawn Fuller has made some mistakes in her life, and she's not proud of the way McDermott Boyd found her off the road one day last year. She's spent a hard year wrestling with her choices and trying to fix them, glad for McDermott's acceptance and friendship. He lost his wife years ago, done his best with his daughter, and now he's ready to move on. **Can McDermott help Dawn find a way past her former mistakes and down a path that leads to love, family, and happiness?**

The Detective's Date: A Fuller Family Novel - Brush Creek Cowboys Romance (Book 4): Dahlia Reid is one of the best detectives Brush Creek and the surrounding towns has ever had. She's given up on the idea of marriage—and pleasing her mother—and has dedicated herself fully to her job. Which is great, since one of the most 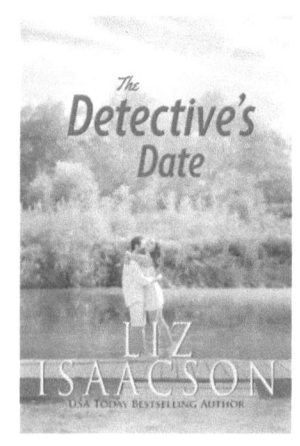 perplexing cases of her career has come to town. Kyler Fuller thinks he's finally ready to move past the woman who ghosted him years ago. He's cut his hair, and he's ready to start dating. Too bad every woman he's been out with is about as interesting as a lamppost—until Dahlia. He finds her beautiful, her quick wit a breath of fresh air, and her intelligence sexy. **Can Kyler and Dahlia use their faith to find a way through the obstacles threatening to keep them apart?**

The Paramedic's Partner: A Fuller Family Novel - Brush Creek Cowboys Romance (Book 5): Jazzy Fuller has always been overshadowed by her prettier, more popular twin, Fabiana. Fabi meets paramedic Max Robinson at the park and sets a date with him only to come down with the flu. So she convinces Jazzy to cut her hair and take her place on the date. And the spark between Jazzy and Max is hot and instant...if only he knew she wasn't her sister, Fabi.

Max drives the ambulance for the town of Brush Creek with is partner Ed Moon, and neither of them have been all that lucky in love. Until Max suggests to who he thinks is Fabi that they should double with Ed and Jazzy. They do, and Fabi is smitten with the steady, strong Ed Moon. **As each twin falls further and further in love with their respective paramedic, it becomes obvious they'll need to come clean about the switcheroo sooner rather than later...or risk losing their hearts.**

The Chief's Catch: A Fuller Family Novel - Brush Creek Cowboys Romance (Book 6): Berlin Fuller has struck out with the dating scene in Brush Creek more times than she cares to admit. When she makes a deal with her friends that they can choose the next man she goes out with, she didn't dream they'd pick surly Cole Fairbanks, the new Chief of Police.

His friends call him the Beast and challenge him to complete ten dates that summer or give up his bonus check. When Berlin approaches him, stuttering about the deal with her friends and claiming they don't actually have to go out, he's intrigued. As the summer passes, Cole finds himself burning both ends of the candle to keep up with his job and his new relationship. **When he unleashes the Beast one time too many, Berlin will have to decide if she can tame him or if she should walk away.**

Books in the Christmas in Coral Canyon Romance series

Graham (Book 1): Graham Whittaker returns to Coral Canyon a few days after Christmas—after the death of his father. He takes over the energy company his dad built from the ground up and buys a high-end lodge to live in—only a mile from the home of his once-best friend, Laney McAllister. They were best friends once, but Laney's always entertained feelings for him, and spending so much time with him while they make Christmas memories puts her heart in danger of getting broken again...

Eli (Book 2): Since the death of his wife a few years ago, Eli Whittaker has been running from one job to another, unable to find somewhere for him and his son to settle. Meg Palmer is Stockton's nanny, and she comes with her boss, Eli, to the lodge, her long-time crush on the man no different in Wyoming than it was on the beach. When she confesses her feelings for him and gets nothing in return, she's crushed, embarrassed, and unsure if she can stay in Coral Canyon for Christmas. Then Eli starts to show some feelings for her too...

Andrew (Book 3): Andrew Whittaker is the public face for the Whittaker Brothers' family energy company, and with his older brother's robot about to be announced, he needs a press secretary to help him get everything ready and tour the state to make the announcements. When he's hit by a protest sign being carried by the company's biggest opponent, Rebecca Collings, he learns with a few clicks that she has the background they need. He offers her the job of press secretary when she thought she was going to be arrested, and not only because the spark between them in so hot Andrew can't see straight.

Can Becca and Andrew work together and keep their relationship a secret? Or will hearts break in this classic romance retelling reminiscent of *Two Weeks Notice*?

Beau (Book 4): Beau Whittaker has watched his brothers find love one by one, but every attempt he's made has ended in disaster. Lily Everett has been in the spotlight since childhood and has half a dozen platinum records with her two sisters. She's taking a break from the brutal music industry and hiding out in Wyoming while her ex-husband continues to cause trouble for her. When she hears of Beau Whittaker and what he offers his clients, she wants to meet him. Beau is instantly attracted to Lily, but he tried a relationship with his last client that left a scar that still hasn't healed...

Can Lily use the spirit of Christmas to discover what matters most? Will Beau open his heart to the possibility of love with someone so different from him?

Todd (Book 5): Todd Christopherson has just retired from the professional rodeo circuit and returned to his hometown of Coral Canyon. Problem is, he's got no family there anymore, no land, and no job. Not that he needs a job--he's got plenty of money from his illustrious career riding bulls.

Then Todd gets thrown during a routine horseback ride up the canyon, and his only support as he recovers physically is the beautiful Violet Everett. She's no nurse, but she does the best she can for the handsome cowboy. **Will she lose her heart to the billionaire bull rider? Can Todd trust that God led him to Coral Canyon...and Vi?**

Liam (Book 6): Rose Everett isn't sure what to do with her life now that her country music career is on hold. After all, with both of her sisters in Coral Canyon, and one about to have a baby, they're not making albums anymore.

Liam Murphy has been working for Doctors Without Borders, but he's back in the US now, and looking to start a new clinic in Coral Canyon, where he spent his summers.

When Rose wins a date with Liam in a bachelor auction, their relationship blooms and grows quickly. **Can Liam and Rose find a solution to their problems that doesn't involve one of them leaving Coral Canyon with a broken heart?**

Finn (Book 7): Her sons want her to be happy, but she's too old to be set up on a blind date...isn't she?

Amanda Whittaker has been looking for a second chance at love since the death of her husband several years ago. Finley Barber is a cowboy in every sense of the word. Born and raised on a racehorse farm in Kentucky, he's since moved to Dog Valley and started his own breeding stable for champion horses. He hasn't dated in years, and everything about Amanda makes him nervous.

Will Amanda take the leap of faith required to be with Finn? Or will he become just another boyfriend who doesn't make the cut?

Zach (Book 8): When Celia Abbott-Armstrong runs into a gorgeous cowboy at her best friend's wedding, she decides she's ready to start dating again.

But the cowboy is Zach Zuckerman, and the Zuckermans and Abbotts have been at war for generations.

Can Zach and Celia find a way to reconcile their family's differences so they can have a future together?

Colton (Book 1): All the maid at Whiskey Mountain Lodge wants for her birthday is a handsome cowboy billionaire. And Colton can make that wish come true—if only he hadn't escaped to Coral Canyon after being left at the altar...

Wes (Book 2): She broke up with him to date another man...who broke her heart. He's a former CEO with nothing to do who can't get her out of his head. Can Wes and Bree find a way toward happily-ever-after at Whiskey Mountain Lodge?

Gray (Book 3): She's best friends with the single dad cowboy's brother and has watched two friends find love with the sexy new cowboys in town. When Gray Hammond comes to Whiskey Mountain Lodge with his son, will Elise finally get her own happily-ever-after with one of the Hammond brothers?

Cy (Book 4): A cowboy billionaire beast, his new manager, and the Christmas traditions that soften his heart and bring them together.

Ames (Book 5): A cowboy billionaire cop who's a stickler for rules, the woman he pulls over when he's not even on duty, and the personal mandates he has to break to keep her in his life...

Second Chance Ranch: A Three Rivers Ranch Romance™ (Book 1): After his deployment, injured and discharged Major Squire Ackerman returns to Three Rivers Ranch, wanting to forgive Kelly for ignoring him a decade ago. He'd like to provide the stable life she needs, but with old wounds opening and a ranch on the brink of financial collapse, it will take patience and faith to make their second chance possible.

Third Time's the Charm: A Three Rivers Ranch Romance™ (Book 2): First Lieutenant Peter Marshall has a truckload of debt and no way to provide for a family, but Chelsea helps him see past all the obstacles, all the scars. With so many unknowns, can Pete and Chelsea develop the love, acceptance, and faith needed to find their happily ever after?

Fourth and Long: A Three Rivers Ranch Romance™ (Book 3): Commander Brett Murphy goes to Three Rivers Ranch to find some rest and relaxation with his Army buddies. Having his ex-wife show up with a seven-year-old she claims is his son is anything but the R&R he craves. Kate needs to make amends, and Brett needs to find forgiveness, but are they too late to find their happily ever after?

Fifth Generation Cowboy: A Three Rivers Ranch Romance™ (Book 4): Tom Lovell has watched his friends find their true happiness on Three Rivers Ranch, but everywhere he looks, he only sees friends. Rose Reyes has been bringing her daughter out to the ranch for equine therapy for months, but it doesn't seem to be working. Her challenges with Mari are just as frustrating as ever. Could Tom be exactly what Rose needs? Can he remove his friendship blinders and find love with someone who's been right in front of him all this time?

Sixth Street Love Affair: A Three Rivers Ranch Romance™ (Book 5): After losing his wife a few years back, Garth Ahlstrom thinks he's ready for a second chance at love. But Juliette Thompson has a secret that could destroy their budding relationship. Can they find the strength, patience, and faith to make things work?

The Seventh Sergeant: A Three Rivers Ranch Romance™ (Book 6): Life has finally started to settle down for Sergeant Reese Sanders after his devastating injury overseas. Discharged from the Army and now with a good job at Courage Reins, he's finally found happiness—until a horrific fall puts him right back where he was years ago: Injured and depressed. Carly Watters, Reese's new veteran care coordinator, dislikes small towns almost as much as she loathes cowboys. But she finds herself faced with both when she gets assigned to Reese's case. Do they have the humility and faith to make their relationship more than professional?

Eight Second Ride: A Three Rivers Ranch Romance™ (Book 7): Ethan Greene loves his work at Three Rivers Ranch, but he can't seem to find the right woman to settle down with. When sassy yet vulnerable Brynn Bowman shows up at the ranch to recruit him back to the rodeo circuit, he takes a different approach with the barrel racing champion. His patience and newfound faith pay off when a friendship--and more--starts with Brynn. But she wants out of the rodeo circuit right when Ethan wants to rejoin. Can they find the path God wants them to take and still stay together?

The Ninth Inning: A Three Rivers Ranch Romance™ (Book 8): The Christmas season has never felt like such a burden to boutique owner Andrea Larsen. But with Mama gone and the holidays upon her, Andy finds herself wishing she hadn't been so quick to judge her former boyfriend, cowboy Lawrence Collins. Well, Lawrence hasn't forgotten about Andy either, and he devises a plan to get her out to the ranch so they can reconnect. Do they have the faith and humility to patch things up and start a new relationship?

Ten Days in Town: A Three Rivers Ranch Romance™ (Book 9): Sandy Keller is tired of the dating scene in Three Rivers. Though she owns the pancake house, she's looking for a fresh start, which means an escape from the town where she grew up. When her older brother's best friend, Tad Jorgensen, comes to town for the holidays, it is a balm to his weary soul. A helicopter tour guide who experienced a near-death experience, he's looking to start over too--but in Three Rivers. Can Sandy and Tad navigate their troubles to find the path God wants them to take--and discover true love--in only ten days?

Eleven Year Reunion: A Three Rivers Ranch Romance™ (Book 10): Pastry chef extraordinaire, Grace Lewis has moved to Three Rivers to help Heidi Ackerman open a bakery in Three Rivers. Grace relishes the idea of starting over in a town where no one knows about her failed cupcakery. She doesn't expect to run into her old high school boyfriend, Jonathan Carver. A carpenter working at Three Rivers Ranch, Jon's in town against his will. But with Grace now on the scene, Jon's thinking life in Three Rivers is suddenly looking up. But with her focus on baking and his disdain for small towns, can they make their eleven year reunion stick?

The Twelfth Town: A Three Rivers Ranch Romance™ (Book 11): Newscaster Taryn Tucker has had enough of life on-screen. She's bounced from town to town before arriving in Three Rivers, completely alone and completely anonymous--just the way she now likes it. She takes a job cleaning at Three Rivers Ranch, hoping for a chance to figure out who she is and where God wants her. When she meets happy-go-lucky cowhand Kenny Stockton, she doesn't expect sparks to fly. Kenny's always been "the best friend" for his female friends, but the pull between him and Taryn can't be denied. Will they have the courage and faith necessary to make their opposite worlds mesh?

Lucky Number Thirteen: A Three Rivers Ranch Romance™ (Book 12): Tanner Wolf, a rodeo champion ten times over, is excited to be riding in Three Rivers for the first time since he left his philandering ways and found religion. Seeing his old friends Ethan and Brynn is therapuetic--until a terrible accident lands him in the hospital. With his rodeo career over, Tanner thinks maybe he'll stay in town--and it's not just because his nurse, Summer Hamblin, is the prettiest woman he's ever met. But Summer's the queen of first dates, and as she looks for a way to make a relationship with the transient rodeo star work Summer's not sure she has the fortitude to go on a second date. Can they find love among the tragedy?

The Curse of February Fourteenth: A Three Rivers Ranch Romance™ (Book 13): Cal Hodgkins, cowboy veterinarian at Bowman's Breeds, isn't planning to meet anyone at the masked dance in small-town Three Rivers. He just wants to get his bachelor friends off his back and sit on the sidelines to drink his punch. But when he sees a woman dressed in gorgeous butterfly wings and cowgirl boots with blue stitching, he's smitten. Too bad she runs away from the dance before he can get her name, leaving only her boot behind...

Fifteen Minutes of Fame: A Three Rivers Ranch Romance™ (Book 14): Navy Richards is thirty-five years of tired—tired of dating the same men, working a demanding job, and getting her heart broken over and over again. Her aunt has always spoken highly of the matchmaker in Three Rivers, Texas, so she takes a six-month sabbatical from her high-stress job as a pediatric nurse, hops on a bus, and meets with the matchmaker. Then she meets Gavin Redd. He's handsome, he's hardworking, and he's a cowboy. But is he an Aquarius too? Navy's not making a move until she knows for sure...

Sixteen Steps to Fall in Love: A Three Rivers Ranch Romance™ (Book 15): A chance encounter at a dog park sheds new light on the tall, talented Boone that Nicole can't ignore. As they get to know each other better and start to dig into each other's past, Nicole is the one who wants to run. This time from her growing admiration and attachment to Boone. From her aging parents. From herself.

But Boone feels the attraction between them too, and he decides he's tired of running and ready to make Three Rivers his permanent home. **Can Boone and Nicole use their faith to overcome their differences and find a happily-ever-after together?**

The Sleigh on Seventeenth Street: A Three Rivers Ranch Romance™ (Book 16): A cowboy with skills as an electrician tries a relationship with a down-on-her luck plumber. Can Dylan and Camila make water and electricity play nicely together this Christmas season? Or will they get shocked as they try to make their relationship work?

The First Lady of Three Rivers Ranch: A Three Rivers Ranch Romance™ (Book 17): Heidi Duffin has been dreaming about opening her own bakery since she was thirteen years old. She scrimped and saved for years to afford baking and pastry school in San Francisco. And now she only has one year left before she's a certified pastry chef. Frank Ackerman's father has recently retired, and he's taken over the largest cattle ranch in the Texas Panhandle. A horseman through and through, he's also nearing thirty-one and looking for someone to bring love and joy to a homestead that's been dominated by men for a decade. But when he convinces Heidi to come clean the cowboy cabins, she changes all that. But the siren's call of a bakery is still loud in Heidi's ears, even if she's also seeing a future with Frank. Can she rely on her faith in ways she's never had to before or will their relationship end when summer does?

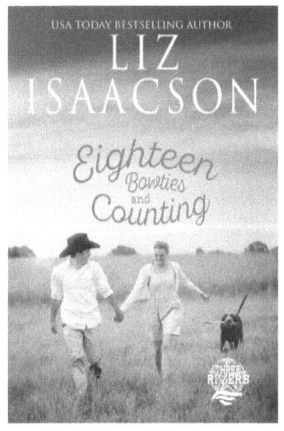

Eighteen Bowties and Counting: A Three Rivers Ranch Romance™ (Book 18): He's her older brother's best friend and completely off-limits. She's got a way with horses...and a heart condition. Can Beau and Charlotte navigate close quarters to find their happily-ever-after?

Last Chance Ranch Romance
Series

Last Chance Ranch (Book 1): A cowgirl down on her luck hires a man who's good with horses and under the hood of a car. Can Hudson fine tune Scarlett's heart as they work together? Or will things backfire and make everything worse at Last Chance Ranch?

Last Chance Cowboy (Book 2): A billionaire cowboy without a home meets a woman who secretly makes food videos to pay her debts...Can Carson and Adele do more than fight in the kitchens at Last Chance Ranch?

Last Chance Wedding (Book 3): A female carpenter needs a husband just for a few days... Can Jeri and Sawyer navigate the minefield of a pretend marriage before their feelings become real?

Last Chance Reunion (Book 4): An Army cowboy, the woman he dated years ago, and their last chance at Last Chance Ranch... Can Dave and Sissy put aside hurt feelings and make their second chance romance work?

Last Chance Lake (Book 5): A former dairy farmer and the marketing director on the ranch have to work together to make the cow cuddling program a success. But can Karla let Cache into her life? Or will she keep all her secrets from him - and keep *him* a secret too?

Last Chance Christmas (Book 6): She's tired of having her heart broken by cowboys. He waited too long to ask her out. Can Lance fix things quickly, or will Amber leave Last Chance Ranch before he can tell her how he feels?

His First Love (Book 1): She broke up with him a decade ago. He's back in town after finishing a degree at MIT, ready to start his job at the family company. Can Hunter and Molly find their way through their pasts to build a future together?

His Second Chance (Book 2): They broke up over twenty years ago. She's lost everything when she shows up at the farm in Ivory Peaks where he works. Can Matt and Gloria heal from their pasts to find a future happily-ever-after with each other?

 **His Third Try (Book 3):** He moved to Ivory Peaks with his daughter to start over after a devastating break-up. She's never had a meaningful relationship with a man, especially a cowboy. Can Boone and Cosette help each other heal enough to build a happily-ever-after...and a family?

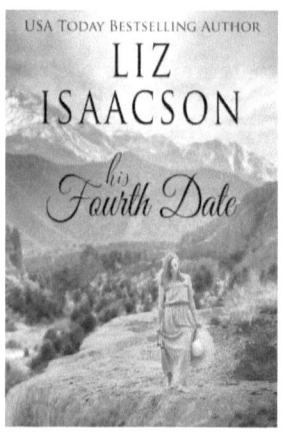

His Fourth Date (Book 4): Their relationship has been nothing but loose goats, a leaking roof, and her complete humiliation after he pays her mortgage so she won't lose her farm. Travis wants to go back in time and start over with Poppy, but he doesn't know how. Can a small town speed-dating event get their second chance off on the right foot?

His Fifth Kiss (Book 5): They once had a few summers together. Now, Michael Hammond is back in town after a devastating injury overseas. He's looking to reset and recover...not to fall in love. But with Gertrude Whettstein also back at the farm, can Gerty and Mike make their second chance romance into a happily-ever-after?

His Sixth Sweetheart (Book 6): She's had a crush on him for decades. He's finally in a place where he feels ready to date the boss's daughter. Can Cord and Jane take their relationship to the next level without getting burned?

His Seventh Stop (Book 7): He's a seasoned cowboy on a delivery mission. She's a resilient hobby farm owner braving the winter storm. Can Keith and Lindsay forge a bond in the heart of a tempest and find love in the calm that follows?

His Eighth Ride (Book 8): Tag has secretly admired Opal from afar. He even went so far as to ask her out, but the timing was all off, and now he's just awkward around his best friend's little sister. Can their unexpected reunion mend the fences between them and finally lead them to the forever love they've been waiting for?

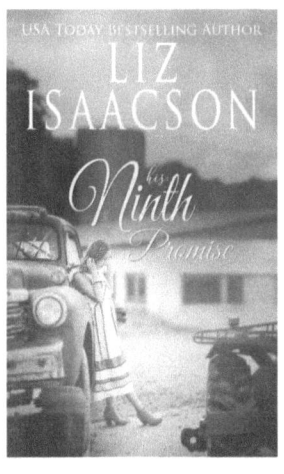

His Ninth Promise (Book 9): At home on the Hammond Family Farm, where gypsy souls and rodeo dreams collide, Tucker's heart has been beating for Bobbie Jo. But with her heart set on a distant love and Tucker searching for something more, their paths seemed destined to cross but never converge. Can he stick it out for another ride if the promise is coming home to Bobbie Jo?

BOOKS IN THE STEEPLE RIDGE ROMANCE SERIES:

Her Billionaire Cowboy (Book 1): Tucker Jenkins has had enough of tall buildings, traffic, and has traded in his technology firm in New York City for Steeple Ridge Horse Farm in rural Vermont. Missy Marino has worked at the farm since she was a teen, and she's always dreamed of owning it. But her ex-husband left her with a truckload of debt, making her fantasies of owning the farm unfulfilled. Tucker didn't come to the country to find a new wife, but he supposes a woman could help him start over in Steeple Ridge. Will Tucker and Missy be able to navigate the shaky ground between them to find a new beginning?

Her Restless Cowboy: A Butters Brothers Novel, Steeple Ridge Romance (Book 2): Ben Buttars is the youngest of the four Buttars brothers who come to Steeple Ridge Farm, and he finally feels like he's landed somewhere he can make a life for himself. Reagan Cantwell is a decade older than Ben and the recreational direction for the town of Island Park. Though Ben is young, he knows what he wants—and that's Rae. Can she figure out how to put what matters most in her life—family and faith—above her job before she loses Ben?

Her Faithful Cowboy: A Butters Brothers Novel, Steeple Ridge Romance (Book 3): Sam Buttars has spent the last decade making sure he and his brothers stay together. They've been at Steeple Ridge for a while now, but with the youngest married and happy, the siren's call to return to his parents' farm in Wyoming is loud in Sam's ears. He'd just go if it weren't for beautiful Bonnie Sherman, who roped his heart the first time he saw her. Do Sam and Bonnie have the faith to find comfort in each other instead of in the people who've already passed?

Her Mistletoe Cowboy: A Butters Brothers Novel, Steeple Ridge Romance (Book 4): Logan Buttars has always been good-natured and happy-go-lucky. After watching two of his brothers settle down, he recognizes a void in his life he didn't know about. Veterinarian Layla Guyman has appreciated Logan's friendship and easy way with animals when he comes into the clinic to get the service dogs. But with his future at Steeple Ridge in the balance, she's not sure a relationship with him is worth the risk. Can she rely on her faith and employ patience to tame Logan's wild heart?

Her Patient Cowboy: A Butters Brothers Novel, Steeple Ridge Romance (Book 5): Darren Buttars is cool, collected, and quiet—and utterly devastated when his girlfriend of nine months, Farrah Irvine, breaks up with him because he wanted her to ride her horse in a parade. But Farrah doesn't ride anymore, a fact she made very clear to Darren. She returned to her childhood home with so much baggage, she doesn't know where to start with the unpacking. Darren's the only Buttars brother who isn't married, and he wants to make Island Park his permanent home—with Farrah. Can they find their way through the heartache to achieve a happily-ever-after together?

Tex (Book 1): He's back in town after a successful country music career. She owns a bordering farm to the family land he wants to buy...and she outbids him at the auction. Can Tex and Abigail rekindle their old flame, or will the issue of land ownership come between them?

Otis (Book 2): He's finished with his last album and looking for a soft place to fall after a devastating break-up. She runs the small town bookshop in Coral Canyon and needs a new boyfriend to get her old one out of her life for good. Can Georgia convince Otis to take another shot at real love when their first kiss was fake?

Morris (Book 3): Morris Young is just settling into his new life as the manager of Country Quad when he attends a wedding. He sees his ex-wife there—apparently Leighann is back in Coral Canyon—along with a little boy who can't be more or less than five years old... Could he be Morris's? And why is his heart hoping for that, and for a reconciliation with the woman who left him because he traveled too much?

Trace (Book 4): He's been accused of only dating celebrities. She's a simple line dance instructor in small town Coral Canyon, with a soft spot for kids...and cowboys. Trace could use some dance lessons to go along with his love lessons... Can he and Everly fall in love with the beat, or will she dance her way right out of his arms?

Blaze (Book 5): He's dark as night, a single dad, and a retired bull riding champion. With all his money, his rugged good looks, and his ability to say all the right things, Faith has no chance against Blaze Young's charms. But she's his complete opposite, and she just doesn't see how they can be together...

...so she ends things with him.

Gabe (Book 6): He's a father's rights advocate lawyer with a sweet little girl. She's fighting for her own daughter. Can Gabe and Hilde find happily-ever-after when they're at such odds with one another?

Jem (Book 7): He's still healing from his vices, and Jem has dedicated everything he has to his two kids. At least he's not mourning his divorce anymore, and in fact, he might be ready to move on. She's his former best friend, and once he breaks his wrist, his nurse. Can Sunny somehow rope this cowboy's heart?

Luke (Book 8): He swore off women when his ex told him he might not be their daughter's father. But a paternity test confirmed he is, and Luke Young has dedicated his life to his little girl and his brothers' band. There hasn't been time for a girlfriend anyway. He's tried here and there, and the women in small-town Coral Canyon are certainly interested in him.

But he's been thinking about his massage therapist for a while now. Can he ask Sterling out when all they've ever been is professional? Oh, and there's the fact that she's seen practically every inch of his body... Awkward, right?

Bryce (Book 9): Bryce Young has been broken and drifting for years. After giving up his son for adoption, he left Coral Canyon and hasn't returned...until now.

Harry (Book 1o): He's looking to make a change from his country music stardom, but the woman who's caught his eye isn't convinced he's permanent enough for her... Can Harry and Belle work out their differences to find a happily-ever-after?

Joey (Book 11): He's a renowned celebrity assistant, now taking over as manager for Country Quad, the legendary band of Young Brothers. She's a young cowgirl trying to find her place in life and her family. Can Joey take a leap of faith and land safely in Adam's arms? Or will small town gossip and expectations crush them both?

About Liz

Liz Isaacson writes inspirational romance, usually set in Texas, or Wyoming, or anywhere else horses and cowboys exist. She lives in Utah, where she writes full-time, takes her two dogs to the park everyday, and eats a lot of veggies while writing. Find her on her website at feelgoodfictionbooks.com

www.ingramcontent.com/pod-product-compliance
Lightning Source LLC
LaVergne TN
LVHW041631060526
838200LV00040B/1532